ROWAN
and the
TRAVELERS

EMILY RODDA

Rowan

and the

TRAVELERS

SCHOLASTIC INC.

New York Toronto London Auckland Sydney
Mexico City New Delhi Hong Kong Buenos Aires

ISBN 0-439-38566-0

Copyright © 1994 by Emily Rodda. Map copyright © 2001 by Lynn Sweat.
All rights reserved. Published by Scholastic Inc., 557 Broadway,
New York, NY 10012, by arrangement with Greenwillow Books, an imprint
of HarperCollins Publishers. SCHOLASTIC and associated logos are
trademarks and/or registered trademarks of Scholastic Inc.

12 11 10 9 8 7 6 5 4 3 2   2 3 4 5 6 7/0

Printed in the U.S.A.   40

First Scholastic printing, September 2002

The text of this book is set in Weiss.

CONTENTS

1 ∾ GOOD NEWS, BAD NEWS

"The Travelers are coming. The Travelers are coming!"

The news spread quickly through the village of Rin. The children shouted it in excitement, their voices ringing through the valley and echoing back from the great Mountain that rose above the town. They shouted it running, running madly down from the hills, past the bukshah fields and the orchard, beside the gardens, and all the way to the village square.

They had seen the three Forerunners flying over the hills, the silken kites to which they clung brilliant against the sky. They knew the carts, the horses, and the chattering, singing people were not far behind.

The Travelers were coming, bringing games and stories, dancing and music, wonderful things to trade. Soon their bright tents would spread, fluttering like huge butterflies, among the yellow slip-daisies on the hills above the village. At night their bonfires would brighten the darkness, and their music would ring through the valley. They would stay a week, or two, or three, and for the children every day would be like a holiday.

"The Travelers are coming!"

Standing by the bukshah pool, watching a butterfly struggle from its cocoon on the branch of a tree, the boy Rowan, keeper of the bukshah, heard the cry. But he had already guessed the news.

Long before the other children spied the Forerunners, he had seen the bukshah raise their heads and look across the valley, to the hills. The big animals were listening to something he could not hear.

"So the Travelers *are* coming?" he said to Star, his favorite of all the great beasts. "You heard their pipes before, didn't you?"

Star stood swaying, looking out to the hills.

"We did not expect to see them this year," Rowan went on, "but it is the season for them. The tadpoles in the stream are growing legs and changing into frogs. The caterpillars are becoming butterflies. And the slip-daisies are in bloom." He sniffled. "As well I know. The pollen makes my nose run."

Star rumbled deep in her throat and shifted her feet restlessly.

"What ails you, Star?" Rowan asked her, scratching her neck under the thick wool. "Be still. All is well."

He looked at Star in puzzlement. All the bukshah had been unsettled lately. And he could not understand why. He had checked them over very carefully. There was no sign of sickness. And yet for days they had seemed nervous and unhappy.

"All is well, Star," he said again.

But Star pawed the ground, pushed at his hand with her heavy head, and refused to be comforted.

"The Travelers are coming!"

Strong Jonn, working in the orchard, heard the cry with surprise, then smiled. The Travelers had come in Rin's direction only twelve months before. He had not expected them again so soon. But he welcomed them. For with the Travelers came their bees.

Soon the bees would be busy in the sweet white blossom of his hoopberry trees. Their hives would begin to overflow with rich, golden hoopberry honey for the Travelers to gather, to eat, and to sell.

But while the bees worked for the Travelers, they would be working for Jonn, too. Bumbling from flower to flower, they would spread the sticky yellow pollen, making sure that fruit would form when the flowers fell. Thanks to the Travelers' bees, Jonn would have a very good harvest in the autumn.

So Jonn was pleased when he heard the children's voices. But he knew others would not be so pleased. For others, the news would be bad.

"The Travelers are coming!"

Bronden the furniture maker heard the cry and frowned, drumming her stubby fingers on the smooth wood of the half-finished table under her hand.

"Slips," she grumbled, kicking her feet in the sawdust on the floor. "Time-wasting, idle, useless Slips!"

She ran her hand over her forehead. She was tired. Tired out. And this—this was the last straw.

The Travelers turned the settled life of the village upside down. They cared nothing for rules, or order, or hard work. They had no settled homes or proper jobs and wanted none. That was why she, and others who thought like her, called the Travelers Slips, after the wild slip-daisies on the hills. Slips made her uncomfortable. They made her angry.

"The Travelers are coming!"

In his little house Timon the teacher heard the cry and sighed over his books. While the Travelers were camping near, the Rin children would fidget and whisper under the Teaching Tree.

Their pockets would bulge with the toys and tricks they had begged or bought from the camp on the hill. Their mouths would be full of honey sweets and chews. Their heads would be buzzing with Travelers' tales and legends.

But still, thought Timon, leaning back in his chair and putting his hands behind his head, this visit might be a blessing. It has been a long, hard winter. The children have been tired and out of sorts lately. The Travelers will cheer them up.

He smiled. By my life, I loved Travelers' tales myself, as a boy, he thought. And if stories of the Valley of Gold, the Giants of Inspray, the Misty Crystal, the Pit of Unrin, and all the rest did not hurt me, then why should they hurt the children now?

Timon considered. Perhaps he could visit the Travelers' camp himself this year. Listen once again to the stories. And perhaps buy a handful of honey chews. It was a long time since he had tasted one of those.

Timon closed his eyes and chuckled sleepily to himself at the thought. His mouth was already watering.

"The Travelers are coming!"

Allun the baker heard the cry as he kneaded dough in his warm kitchen. "Do you hear that, Mother? My father's people are on their way," he called over his shoulder. "You had better stop all that talk of growing old and get your dancing shoes out."

Sara came slowly in from the shop, wiping her hands on her apron.

"I think my dancing days are over, Allun," she said, with a tired smile. "But you had better get your voice in order. For once, we of Rin have a tale to tell the Travelers. As good as any they have ever told us. Our friends will want to hear of your quest to the Mountain. Yours, and Jonn's, and—"

"And young Rowan's most of all," laughed Allun. "But Rowan is much too shy to tell the story himself. So, yes, I will. Who better to surprise the Travelers—since I am half a Traveler myself!"

Sara fingered the thin string of plaited silk that hung around her throat. It was a Traveler wedding necklace.

Long ago, when she was young, Sara had left Rin with a Traveler husband. But her perfect happiness had ended when her man was killed by the invading Zebak during the great War of the Plains. When the land was at peace once more, she had returned to the village with Allun, her only son, then just a boy.

Sara had been glad to see her home again. But she knew that times had often been hard for her half-Traveler child as he grew up in Rin.

It was as though he was caught between two worlds: the free, roaming life of the Travelers, and the peaceful, settled life of his mother's people. Sara's heart had sometimes bled as she saw him struggling to be accepted by those Rin folk who despised and distrusted the Travelers, and who therefore were ready to despise and distrust him, too.

She had not wanted Allun to join the group that had climbed the forbidden Mountain in the autumn. She had feared for him. But now she was glad that he had gone. For on that terrible journey he had found that he had no more weaknesses than the others, the heroes of the village. And those who scorned him had realized it, too.

And more: Allun had brought back from his quest a special gift. A gift that looked as though it would bring riches to the town. So at last he felt he had proved that he was a worthy citizen of Rin. And because of that, he had found a new peace. Surely nothing could destroy it now.

"Why, I wonder, have they returned so soon?" Allun murmured. His merry face had grown thoughtful. "Many in the village will not be pleased to see them here again."

Sara watched her son as he turned back to his work. She listened to the children's voices ringing through the valley. And for the first time a shadow of fear fluttered through her mind. Why *had* the Travelers come again so soon?

Why?

2 ⌇ DARKNESS GATHERS

 In the gardens, Bree and Hanna heard the children's cry and put down their hoes. For them this news was very bad indeed.

"How can this be?" exclaimed Hanna, turning to her husband and wiping the sweat from her forehead. "They *never* come two years in a row."

Bree and Hanna, and the keepers of the Rin gardens before them, had always hated the Travelers' visits. Travelers could move silently, like shadows in the night. New peas, tender herbs—all the best things in the gardens—had a habit of disappearing like magic overnight when Travelers were about.

Others in the village, people like Jonn of the Orchard and Allun the baker, always laughed when the gardeners raged. Even if a few vegetables *had* somehow found their way into Travelers' cooking pots over the years, what did that matter, when the Travelers brought the village so much useful trade and so much pleasure?

Bree spat on the ground in disgust. Perhaps such people would sing a different tune this year. Even the half-Traveler Allun. For after all, it was he who had brought the seed for the new crop to the valley.

Bree looked at the young Mountain berry plants that now filled a quarter of the garden. They were thriving, holding their small, glossy leaves up to the sun and stretching delicate new tendrils out across the brown soil. Perfumed red flowers bloomed along their tiny branches, already weighed down with luscious little red fruits.

A sturdy, fast-growing plant that bloomed and fruited at the same time! Truly the Mountain berry was miraculous, and a precious new crop. A crop that Bree was determined to keep for Rin alone. He thought of Travelers slipping into the gardens by night, plundering his precious bushes, gathering the fruit. . . .

"Thieving Slips!" he burst out. "They must not hear of the Mountain berries, Hanna. They must not!"

She nodded. "We will call a meeting," she said. "We will tell the others of our fears. Then no one will breathe a word. And we will guard the gardens well."

"I stood guard last year," Bree muttered. "And what good did it do?"

"Last year you fell asleep, Bree."

"They put a sleep spell on me! I know it!" Red-faced, Bree scowled in the direction of the hills.

"Nonsense!" snapped Hanna. "Sleep spells! I never heard such rubbish. You sound like Neel the potter, talking childish nonsense like that."

Bree turned away, hunching his shoulders. "We will call a meeting," he mumbled. "Come and wash, Hanna. We do not have much time."

Hanna said nothing. After a moment Bree picked up the hoes and trudged to the toolshed.

Hanna rubbed her eyes. A great wave of tiredness was suddenly rolling over her. She would have given anything to lie down and rest—just for a minute. I am tired out, she thought. I am so tired of working day in, day out. And now this.

She glanced at her husband. He was wearily putting the hoes away and closing the shed door. Poor Bree. What had she been thinking of? She had to keep going, just as he did. Now there was a new problem to be faced. Well, they would face it together.

If all went well, next season there would be Mountain berries in plenty. Then they could rest, and Rin could feast. Trade, too, for no one on the coast had ever tasted this new, delicious fruit. Wealth would be theirs at last.

If all went well.

The bell sounded in the village square. Rowan heard it from the bukshah fields.

"There is a meeting, Star," he said. "I must go. You take care of the herd while I am away."

Star rumbled in her throat and looked out toward the hills.

"The meeting will be about the Travelers, I am sure," Rowan told her. "Jonn will be pleased to see them again. And so will Allun. And Marlie the weaver will be glad, because the Travelers will trade their silk for her warm cloth. But Bronden will be angry. And Bree and Hanna will be *furious*, because the Travelers steal from the gardens."

He smiled guiltily. If Bree and Hanna were not looking, he himself sometimes grabbed a handful of new peas through the fence on his way to the bukshah fields. His animals were very fond of new peas.

Then Rowan remembered the Mountain berries,

and the brightness of the afternoon seemed to dim.
If the Travelers interfered with the Mountain
berries . . .

Star swayed and pawed the ground restlessly.
Rowan forgot his own problems and gripped her
rough mane in concern.

"Be calm," he said, soothing her. "You have nothing to fear."

Star fixed him with her small black eyes and
nudged him with her shoulder. It was as though she
was trying to tell him something. He felt her skin
quiver under the thick wool.

Rowan sighed. Behind him, the butterfly finished
stretching its new wings and flew away, leaving its
hard cocoon hanging empty in the tree. A light,
cool breeze ruffled his hair, carrying with it the
scent of slip-daisies from the hills. His nose began
to run again, and his eyes prickled.

In the village, the bell went on ringing.

Crouched by the fire in her tiny hut, Sheba the
Wise Woman heard the bell through a dream. She
jerked awake and bent to throw sticks on the blaze.
The fire leaped.

"A meeting, is it? You fools!" she croaked, watching the pictures in the flames. "You fools, to chatter on while darkness gathers."

She pressed her hands to her head. The terrifying words that had cried in her mind for so many days circled there, endlessly and without meaning. And with the words, over and over again, were the pictures. . . .

Three kites: yellow, red, and white, against a blue sky. The pale face of a boy she knew—Rowan of the Bukshah. And a golden owl, with glittering green eyes that stared at her, full of knowledge. Commanding her to understand.

There were other pictures, too, lit by flashes of golden light, then shut off by inky blackness. The bukshah fields empty. The village of Rin still and silent. And, most terrifying of all, a heaped bundle of old rags and straggled hair, lying by a dead fire. She herself, in this very room. Helpless. While the enemy . . .

Sheba struggled to her feet. Waking or sleeping, there was no escape. The fire spat and crackled. She backed away from it.

Suddenly she knew what she must do. She must go about her work. She must escape from this place of nightmares. She must go collecting roots on the hills, where the sweet slip-daisies bloomed and the air was clear. There, perhaps, she could think.

As she shuffled from the hut, the bell stopped ringing. The people of Rin were gathered. They were meeting in the square.

"Fools!" Sheba spat. And staggered on her way.

3 ∽ THE FORERUNNERS

"Welcome, friends!"

Jonn's voice sounded loudly on the hills.
He, Marlie the weaver, and Allun the baker
shaded their eyes against the sun as they watched
the three approaching Forerunners raise their arms
in answer to the call. Rowan, standing behind them,
saw the one in the center put something to her lips.

Wherever the Travelers went, the Forerunners
flew before, warning of dangers ahead, signaling
with their tiny reed pipes to tell if the tribe should
halt or go forward. The pipes' sound was pitched
too high for ordinary people to hear. Only the
Travelers, their ears trained over centuries, heard
their messages. The Travelers and, as Rowan had
discovered, the bukshah.

Perhaps other animals heard the pipes, too. Rowan did not know. In fact, the older he grew, the more he realized just how little he did know about the land beyond the valley of Rin.

The Travelers had ranged far and wide over the land for ages past. They knew it as they knew themselves. They were part of it, as were the trees, the rocks, the birds, and the bukshah. Some of the tales told by Ogden, their storyteller and the leader of the tribe, were thousands of years old.

But the people of Rin were newcomers. Barely three hundred years had passed since their ancestors were brought to the coast as warrior slaves of the invading Zebak. It was then that they turned against their masters, joined with the Maris folk and the Travelers to defeat them, and finally traveled inland to find the valley that was now their home.

Three hundred years was as nothing to the Maris folk—and less than nothing to the Travelers, who believed that their tribe had roamed this land since time began.

Yet I do not feel like a newcomer, Rowan thought now, looking down to Rin, with its neat lanes and houses, its bubbling stream, the green-and-brown patchwork of its fields, the hoopberry orchard, and the bukshah straying up toward the hills. This is the only home I know.

"It will not be long now," murmured Jonn to Allun and Marlie. "Let us hope that what we hear will satisfy the worriers below."

He bent and picked the leaf of a slip-daisy, twisting it between his fingers. Rowan knew that the leaf was part of the Welcoming. Slip-daisy leaves were made of three round lobes joined together, as clover leaves were. They were used as a sign of the friendship between the Travelers, the Maris folk, and the people of Rin.

The Forerunners had begun flying low, their bare toes lightly skimming the tips of the grass and flowers. Their kites—one yellow, one red, one white—rippled and flapped in the breeze as the ropes of plaited silk that guided them were pulled tight in agile brown hands.

Rowan drank in the sight greedily. He had never seen the Forerunners so closely before. Three adult Rin Welcomers usually met them alone.

But this time the villagers wanted news quickly. They had decided at their meeting to find out the reason for the Travelers' unexpected visit before discussing the Mountain berry problem further. Rowan was to run to the village with the news as soon as it was given.

"It is my one regret," said Allun, watching the bright kites, "that my mother took me from the Travelers before I was old enough to train as a Forerunner."

"Would you have wished that, Allun?" asked Jonn in some surprise. "It is a rank of honor, I know. But great dangers go with it, surely."

Allun smiled wryly. "You are right, of course," he admitted. "If the Forerunners meet trouble, they meet it alone, while the tribe stays back in safety. That is their duty. But the kites, Jonn! The kites! To fly on the wind is every Traveler child's dearest wish."

As he spoke, the Forerunners' flight slowed to walking pace. Then, with one movement, the three put their feet to the ground. Their kites billowed behind them for a moment, then folded gracefully into thin, trailing sacks of silk. The Forerunners gathered them up unhurriedly, draping the silk over their shoulders as they moved forward to greet the Welcomers.

Jonn held out the slip-daisy leaf. "Welcome, friends," he said again.

Rowan stared at the Forerunners with fascination. They wore clothes of bright silk. Their feet were bare. Their brown hair, threaded with flowers, feathers, and ribbons, fell in tangled curls over their shoulders. They were two boys and a girl, all a little older than he was.

The boys were small boned and slim, like Allun. They looked up at Jonn with dark eyes that danced under slanting brows. The girl was sterner. She was tall—almost as tall as Marlie. Her brows were straight, her eyes a strange light blue. She stepped forward and took the leaf from Jonn.

"I am Zeel, adopted daughter of Ogden the storyteller. The Travelers thank you for your welcome, friends," she said formally. "We will make camp here while it suits your pleasure and will welcome your visits each night after sunset."

These, Rowan knew, were the words that were always said. They meant little. The Travelers made camp anywhere they liked. No one but the Zebak had ever tried to interfere with them. And the Zebak, according to the tales, had regretted it.

He waited for what would come next.

"May we know what brings you here again so soon?" Jonn asked. "Never before have the Travelers visited Rin two years in a row."

The pale eyes never moved from his face. "The idea took our fancy," said Zeel the Forerunner. "We felt the need, and so we came."

"We thought you may need food, or other trade," Jonn persisted. "The winter has been long and hard."

"It has," said the girl smoothly. "And we are always pleased to trade with you, our friends. But our need is no greater than it is in any spring."

"We thought you may have news from the coast," Marlie put in. "News of our enemy stirring, perhaps. We thought you may have come to warn us."

Rowan watched Zeel carefully. Had he seen a flicker deep in those pale eyes?

But she shook her head. "We have no news to tell you," she said.

She is lying, thought Rowan. I can feel it. She is lying. Or, at least, not telling the whole truth.

There was silence on the hill. The Forerunners faced Jonn, Marlie, and Allun calmly. Plainly they had nothing more to say.

"So be it," said Jonn at last. He stepped aside, so that the Forerunners could see Rowan clearly, and turned to him. "Run to the village, then, Rowan, and tell the people what our friends have said. There is no special reason for their visit. The idea simply took their fancy."

Rowan could tell by the way Jonn spoke that he, too, felt that Zeel was holding something back. And he was sure that the three Forerunners were quite aware that the Welcomers had not been fooled. They looked a little startled as they stared at him with unblinking eyes, then looked at one another as though passing an unspoken message.

Rowan wasted no more time but nodded, turned, and ran straight back down the hills toward the village. He knew the people in the square would be anxiously awaiting him. He had no comfort to give them. But there was no point in keeping them waiting. And, besides, he wanted to get back to the bukshah.

From the hilltop he could see that the herd was still moving along the stream, every moment straying farther and farther from the village. A fence must have been trodden down. He did not want the beasts to get too far away. Even now it would take him a long time to coax them back to their fields.

He began to pant with the effort of running. Angrily he rubbed at his blocked-up nose and puffy eyes and wished for the millionth time that he was as strong as other boys his age.

He wished it every time he saw Jiller, his mother, trudging behind the plow that turned the soil in their fields. He wished it every time he saw her back bend under a load of grain. At his age he should be able to take his dead father's place to help her—at least in part.

But when he ventured to say this to her, she only smiled. "Strength I have for myself, Rowan," she would say. "And one day you will be big enough to help me more in the fields. For now, you help me in every other way. Let that be enough for you, as it is for me."

The cheeky-faced yellow daisies bowed their heads under his flying feet and then sprang up again behind him. Pollen filled the air in a pale golden cloud. Rowan sneezed as he ran. His eyes watered so that he could hardly see.

Wrinkling his nose, he reached into his pocket and pulled out a small green bottle. He held his breath and took a sip. The strong, horrible-tasting medicine flooded his mouth. He coughed and gasped, forcing himself to swallow.

The medicine was vile. And worse, to him, because it came from Sheba. He shuddered to think that her bony hands had gathered the slip-daisy roots from which the brew was made and stirred the pot in which it simmered.

He was sure the old woman cackled with laughter as she poured the potion into bottles. He was the only person in the village who had to take it, and he had long ago decided that Sheba made it especially foul-tasting for him on purpose. That was the sort of cruel joke she enjoyed.

With relief he saw the shadows of a grove of trees ahead. Soon he would be out of the slip-daisies, and the medicine would start doing its work in a few moments. With luck, then, the sneezes and sniffles would leave him in peace for a while.

He slowed to a walk and began threading through the trees. His streaming eyes, used to the bright sunlight, blinked blindly in the shady dimness. He had to feel his way.

And so it was that at first he did not see the humped shape rising in front of him. He did not shrink back in time to avoid the bony arm that shot out to bar his way. He did not twist quickly enough to stop the iron-hard fingers from gripping his shoulder, forcing him to stop.

Rowan shrieked in shock and fear. The figure before him began to laugh. It was a frightful, jeering laugh. All too familiar.

It was Sheba.

4 ∽ THE RHYME

 "So, Rowan of the Bukshah," the old woman said, tightening her grip on Rowan's shoulder. "Where are you going in such a hurry?"

"To the village," Rowan answered timidly. He felt his nose start to run again, and sniffed.

"You need another dose of my spring potion, boy," Sheba said softly. "Your nose is running like the stream."

She pointed to the bulging bag at her feet. "I have the slip-daisy roots here. I have walked all the way to the hills to pull them. It is hard on my poor old bones. Tonight I will brew the potion. Is that not good? Are you not grateful to old Sheba?"

Rowan scowled. The taste of the medicine was

still foul in his mouth. He looked at Sheba's bag. It was stuffed to overflowing. Enough for a cauldron of the hideous stuff.

Sheba's fingers pinched his shoulder. "Are you not grateful?" she repeated.

Rowan nodded dumbly. What does she want of me? he thought.

Sheba pushed her face close to his. Her skin was gray. She smelled of ashes and bitter herbs. Her hair swung like greasy ropes around her shoulders.

"Why have the Travelers come to the valley, Rowan of the Bukshah?" Her voice was urgent and low. "You must know. In the vision your face is clear when all else is a mystery. Why have they come again so soon? Tell me! Tell me! It may be the key."

"They—they say they have no special reason," stammered Rowan, trying to pull back. The vision? The key? What did she mean?

Her lips drew back from her long yellow teeth in a snarl. "Lies!" Her eyes searched his. They were like black holes in her face. They seemed to burn into him. He felt his head beginning to spin. But he could not turn away.

Finally she nodded. Her eyelids drooped. "So," she mumbled. "Not your lies, but theirs, then, Rowan of the Bukshah." She pushed him roughly aside. "So I was wrong. You are of no use to me. Get out of my sight!"

"What is the matter?" Rowan burst out. Sheba terrified him, but he had to know what all this meant.

She picked up her heavy sack and began to shuffle away.

"Do not go!" Rowan called. "Sheba! How do you know the Forerunners lied? Is there some danger threatening us? Please tell me. You *must* tell me!"

She spun around, baring her teeth at him. "I *must* do nothing, boy," she cried, her voice cracking with sudden fury. "Who are you to order me? Do you think that because the foolish villagers think you are a hero you can tell me what to do? Pah!"

Her eyes narrowed. She seemed filled with a rage that Rowan could not understand. "I know you for what you are, Rowan of the Bukshah," she said. "Skinny rabbit! Weakling, runny-nosed child, scared of your own shadow! No use to your mother in her need. No use to me. No use to anyone. Run away and snivel in the bukshah fields. It is all you are good for!"

Rowan shrank back as if he had been struck. Her words echoed his inmost thoughts. She was right. He was no use to anyone, whatever people said. His face burned. He turned to run. To run away from her hateful voice and spiteful face.

But as he turned, he saw the Mountain, rising dark and secret above the trees. And he remembered the great lesson he had learned there. The lesson the six heroes with him had learned, too. The lesson none of them would ever forget.

He swung around again.

"Only fools do not fear, Sheba. You said that once, and it is true. I know I am not a hero. But I know I can face fear if I must. And now I can face you, and ask again, what ails you? What trouble do you feel, for Rin?"

She stared at him. "The Mountain has taught you well," she said slowly. She looked up at the jagged rocks, the icy tip where snow gleamed in the slowly sinking sun. The jeering look that had veiled her face had dropped away. And underneath it there was something else. Fear!

Rowan's heart leaped in terror. What thing could be so dreadful that it would bring fear to Sheba's face?

"What is it?" he cried.

She shook her head. "I do not know," she said hopelessly. "I do not know. I only know my dreams. The pictures. The words that haunt me, night and

day. The enemy is coming again. The wheel is turning. And this time—this time—"

"What pictures? What words?" Rowan demanded.
"Tell me!"

Suddenly Sheba's hands began to quiver. Then the
shuddering spread until her whole body was trembling as though with a terrible fever. Her eyes rolled
back in her head. The whites gleamed horribly in the
shadows of the trees. Her mouth gaped open.

Rowan sprang forward and grabbed her arm. He
shook it violently. "Speak!" he shouted. "Sheba!"

The gaping mouth began to move. The croaking
chant began.

"Beneath soft looks the evil burns,
And slowly round the old wheel turns.
The same mistakes, the same old pride,
The priceless armor cast aside.
The secret enemy is here.
It hides in darkness, fools beware!
For day by day its power grows,
And when at last its face it shows,
Then past and present tales will meet—
The evil circle is complete. . . ."

The voice trailed off in a bubbling groan. The
old woman swayed. Rowan staggered as he tried to

hold her, to stop her from crumpling to the ground. His throat felt as though it was being gripped by an icy hand.

What did this mean? Sheba's words ran around and around in his mind as he searched for an answer.

The rhyme was about treachery. Betrayal. And it was not a warning for the future. Or not all. Rowan's breath caught in his chest.

The secret enemy is here. The secret enemy . . . is here.

5 ~ DISAGREEMENT

 Cross faces turned to Rowan as he stumbled at last into the village square.

"Where have you *been*, Rowan?" asked his mother. "We have been waiting so long!"

"So *long*!" repeated his little sister, Annad. She put her small hands on her hips and glared at him, waiting for his explanation.

"I . . . met Sheba in the trees," Rowan said hesitantly. "She . . . hindered me."

There was a murmur from the crowd. Sheba was necessary to the village, because she made potions that healed all manner of ills. But she was feared by many as a witch, and disliked by others because of her bad temper and wicked tongue.

"What did she want?" asked Neel the potter.

"Forget her!" ordered old Lann. "Tell us the news from the hills. Tell us now, quickly!" She banged her stick on the ground.

The oldest person in the village, Lann had once also been its greatest fighter. Now she needed her cane to walk, but her mind and her voice were as strong as ever. And she did not like to be kept waiting.

Rowan did not know what to do. Should he tell what Sheba had said? Should he say that he thought the Forerunners had been lying to Jonn?

He looked around the ring of faces in the square. Some people, like Neel the potter, were anxious. Some, like Bronden, Bree, and Hanna, were suspicious. Some, like Solla the sweets maker, were excited. Some, like Val and Ellis from the mill, were merely curious.

Rowan knew how those faces would change if he repeated the rhyme he had heard in the trees. He did not feel certain that he could deal with the fear, anger, and panic that would sweep through the crowd.

"Well?" Bronden's voice rang through the silence.

Rowan made his decision. He would wait until he had had a chance to talk this over with his mother and Strong Jonn, in private. They would know what was best to do. Sheba's words sounded terrifying, but it was possible that she had been playing a trick on him, for spite. For now, he would just repeat the message he had been given on the hill.

"The Forerunners said that the Travelers have no special reason for this visit," he said. "They said that the idea simply took their fancy."

Lann's eyes narrowed, but she said nothing.

Bronden snorted in disgust. "It took their *fancy* to waste our time and eat our food!" she said. "How excellent it must be to be able to have such fancies!"

"They invite us to their camp tonight, and every night they are here, should we care to join them," Rowan went on.

Several adults, and all the children, cheered.

Bronden scowled. "Well, I for one, certainly do not care to join them," she said.

"Nor we," said Bree, glowering at Rowan as if he was at fault. "And all who *do* want to waste their precious time visiting that nest of thieves should remember what we have decided. Not a word of the Mountain berries must be breathed in a Traveler's hearing."

"For certain they know of them already, Bree,"

growled mighty Val the miller. "For why else have they come? This talk of fancies makes no sense." Her twin brother, Ellis, nodded slowly in agreement.

Again there was a murmuring in the crowd. And this time it was an angry sound.

"Nevertheless," said old Lann, "we will hold our tongues. If we are shutting the gate after the bukshah has already strayed, so be it. It is better to be careful than to be sorry. And as well as keeping our mouths shut, we must keep the Travelers out of the gardens at all costs."

"The gardens are not the only places where the berry bushes can be found," Timon reminded her. "Allun and the rest of the Seven who climbed the Mountain have bushes of their own. The birds have feasted on their berries and have spread the seed. New plants are popping up everywhere. More every day. The village is already sweet with their scent." He waved his hand around the square.

"Then we must tell the Slips they are not welcome in the village," said Bree. "They must stay in their camp on the hills."

"We cannot do that, Bree," Timon objected. "The Travelers are our friends, and our allies in time of trouble."

"I agree. We cannot afford to anger the Travelers," Jiller said quietly. "We have fought the Zebak together in the past and may need to do so again one day. We need their friendship."

"And they need ours." Old Lann held her head high. "So they will have to abide by what we say, Jiller. For good or ill. This matter is too important for us to let weakness guide us."

Bree, Hanna, and Bronden nodded in agreement. So did many others.

"So it is decided," said Lann curtly. "It will be done."

Jiller made a small sound of irritation and dismay. Timon looked very grave.

They were not the only ones who would think the decision a foolish one. Rowan could imagine what Allun, Marlie, and Jonn would say when they heard that the Travelers were to be barred from the village.

He turned and began to walk away from the square. The meeting was making him uncomfortable. And he had to see to the bukshah. Soon the sun would slip behind the Mountain and the valley would begin to grow dark and chill. It was important that he return them to their fields before then.

"Rowan, where are you going?" called Annad. She ran up to him and tugged at his hand. "We must go home so we can be ready for dinner early. Jonn is coming to eat with us. Then afterward we can all go to the Travelers' camp together. Mother says."

"I have to go to the bukshah fields first, Annad," Rowan told her. "Star and the others strayed while I was on the hills."

"Why?" the little girl asked.

Rowan tried to smile. "Maybe, like the Travelers, the idea just took their fancy," he said. "But don't worry, Annad. If bringing the beasts home takes too long, I will miss dinner and meet you and Mother and Jonn at the camp. You tell Mother for me. All right?"

She nodded and ran back to the crowd.

Rowan began walking toward the fields. He turned once and saw Annad waving to him. He waved back, then went on his way. What a funny little girl she is, he thought. Always asking why.

Why is the sky blue? Why can't I stay up all night? Why do tadpoles eat weed, and frogs eat insects? Why don't the clouds fall down? Why have the bukshah strayed?

Rowan reached the bukshah pool. There were no beasts in sight at all. With a sigh he began to trudge along the stream.

Why *had* the bukshah strayed, today of all days? There was plenty of new grass in the fields. There was plenty of water. The bukshah never moved far from their pool. But today they had. Just when Rowan wanted to get home with all speed. Sheba's terrible chant was weighing him down. Cruel joke or not, he wanted to share it with his mother and Jonn, and relieve himself of the burden of carrying it alone.

He squinted ahead and saw the bukshah in the far distance. They were still moving down the stream. He quickened his steps.

Life in Rin goes on day by day, unchanging, he thought. And then three strange, worrying things happen all at once. The Travelers arrive, Sheba becomes afraid—or pretends to—and now the bukshah stray. It is bad luck.

Then he frowned.

Was it just bad luck? Or were all three things somehow related?

The sun dipped behind the Mountain. The light dimmed. Rowan shivered. Again Sheba's words were ringing in his brain.

The enemy is here. . . . The enemy is—HERE.

6 ∽ THE VALLEY OF GOLD

"And so the Giants of Inspray fought on the Mountain side, to see which one of them would have the fabled Valley of Gold for himself. For six long days and six long nights they fought. The sound of their shouting was like a furious hurricane, and the clash of their weapons was like a thousand cymbals, and the stamping of their feet was like thunder. And still neither would give in. . . ."

Ogden the storyteller sat by his fire telling his story. Around him clustered many children—children of Rin, and Traveler children, too. For though the Traveler children had heard Ogden's stories time and again, they never tired of them.

Behind them, in the shadows, stood taller figures.

These were the Rin adults who had been drawn to Ogden's campfire. Rowan could see Timon the teacher there, among the rest. Maise, the keeper of the books, stood with him. And there was Allun, too, with Sara, and Marlie, and Solla the sweets maker.

The adults might laugh afterward at the Travelers' tales. They might say the stories Ogden told were not truth but legend, cleverly brought to life. Still, now they would be listening as carefully as anyone else.

Rowan knew that his mother and Strong Jonn of the Orchard were in the crowd as well, for Annad sat beside him now, at the fire. He had not had time to see or speak to them. He had come straight to the camp from the bukshah field.

It had taken hours to see the beasts safely home. When he had finally caught up with the herd, he had needed to speak softly to Star for a long time before she had obeyed him and led the others back to Rin. Then he had mended as best he could the gate they had pushed open to start their wanderings.

He hoped they would settle to sleep now. They could easily break the gate down again if they chose. Star had still seemed restless, but surely she would not try to roam again, in the dark.

Ogden's voice rose, breaking into Rowan's

thoughts. The storyteller's tale was reaching its climax.

"For six days and nights the earth of the Mountain side was trampled and bloodstained. For six days and nights the grass was torn, the trees were battered. For six days and nights the air was filled with the terrible sounds of the giants' fury and the foul smells of the giants' sweat and hatred. And then, as the seventh day dawned, and the battle still raged, it was as though the Mountain cried, 'No more!'

"The ground trembled. Great cracks and pits opened in the land, and smoke and flame rose up to cloud the sky.

"Huge rocks fell crashing from the Mountain top, beating at the giants, tearing down the trees, tumbling down to pile one upon the other around the Valley of Gold. And the people in the Valley were terrified. They cried and clung to one another, thinking that now indeed their last hours had come."

Ogden looked around at the wide eyes of the children sitting at his feet. The wood of his campfire popped and spat. Under his beaky nose his lips curved into a smile. His voice dropped to a murmur.

"And then, at last, the fighting stopped. The smoke and dust cleared. The giants lay dying on the

Mountain side, their bodies broken by the rocks the Mountain had flung at them in its anger. They looked down with glazed eyes, seeking one last glimpse of the beautiful place each had wanted for his own.

"And then they groaned. They howled. They shook their battered fists in helpless rage and pain. For all they could see below were great piles of stones and yawning pits that scarred the earth. The golden prize over which they had fought, in a fury that had been their deaths, was gone from their sight. Gone from the sight of all who would threaten it. Gone forever. Gone, gone, gone . . ."

Ogden's voice dropped away to nothing.

"Oh, no!" whispered Annad, who had not heard the story before. She clenched her fists. "Those wicked giants destroyed the Valley of Gold. The falling rocks covered it. They crashed down and killed all the good, wise people. They buried the jeweled paths, and the silver spring, and the fruits and birds and little white horses and—"

Rowan took her hand. "Shhh, Annad. Listen," he said softly.

Ogden nodded, his black eyes gleaming in the firelight.

"The giants died cursing and weeping. They

cursed one another, and they cursed the Mountain. They wept for the loss of the brightest treasure in the land. But they did not know the Mountain's secret."

He paused. "Do you?" he asked.

The children around him, even those who had heard the story over and over again, shook their heads wordlessly. They wanted Ogden to tell the end.

He leaned forward. His voice was as gentle as the evening breeze now.

"Then I will tell you," he said. "The Valley of Gold was *not* destroyed by the rain of stones. Even as its people clung together, terrified and fearing death, they saw that a miracle was taking place. No rocks were falling into the Valley."

Rowan felt Annad's hand tighten in his. Ogden's soft voice went on.

"While all around it the earth cracked open and huge rocks piled up in heaps, the Valley of Gold remained secure and protected. And when the fall had ended, great new hills of Mountain stone had risen up around it, and the hideous Pit of Unrin, crawling with evil and death, barred the way to its entrance. So the people knew that now their home was safe forever from prying eyes and greedy hands. And they could live on in peace and happiness, without fear."

Annad could not contain herself. "So the Valley of Gold is still there, beyond the Mountain?" she squeaked. "And the people, and the white horses, and the painted houses, and the silver spring, and . . ."

Ogden smiled at her. "As I told you, young one," he said. "But from that day to this, no outsider has ever seen it. Even the Travelers, the great friends of the Valley's people in ages past, do not know where it lies. For the Travelers were doing battle with the Zebak on the coast when the Giants of Inspray fought and died.

"Many foolish souls, those who only believe what they can see, say it exists no more," he went on. "Some say, indeed, that the Valley of Gold never existed at all! But I know it did, and does. And so, now, do you."

Ogden leaned back and folded his hands. Annad relaxed, breathing a sigh of pleasure and contentment.

Rowan wondered yet again about the power of Ogden the storyteller. His words could hold you in a spell, a spell as powerful as any spun with special herbs picked in moonlight or read from an ancient book. Rowan had heard the story of the Valley of Gold several times before. But every time was like the first.

Even now, with all the other things that were filling his mind, the spell had worked on him. Again his mind was filled with wonder. Again he almost believed in the fabled Valley of Gold.

He closed his eyes as Ogden's voice whispered in his memory. "The Valley of Gold . . . a wondrous place, filled with light, and life, and laughter . . . the silver spring, bubbling cool and fresh from beneath the earth . . . bright colored lanterns in the trees . . . beautiful people, tall and strong, wise and good . . . flowers and fruits of every kind, spilling across the paths of gleaming gems that wound between the gardens . . . small white horses, saddled with silk . . . houses painted with beautiful patterns, each one different . . . before each house, a golden bird—an owl with emerald eyes . . ."

Almost, Rowan believed. Almost, he believed that out there, beyond Rin, beyond the Mountain, lay a place of peace and beauty, lost and hidden from prying eyes. Waiting, just waiting . . .

"The Valley of Gold," Annad said softly, her face radiant. "The Valley of Gold."

7 ～ ALLUN TELLS
A TALE

There was a stir in the crowd, and Rowan looked up, his dream interrupted. Allun was stepping forward.

"And now, Ogden," he was saying with a smile. "We of Rin have a story for *you*, if you will listen. It is a new story. A story of great courage."

Rowan's heart thudded. He hadn't known this was going to happen. He felt his face beginning to grow hot. Annad nudged him proudly.

The storyteller looked up in mild surprise. The firelight danced upon his hair. "I will listen with pleasure, Allun," he said mockingly.

He winked at the Traveler children at his feet. "Now what great story do the Rin folk have for us, do you suppose?" he cried. "Did a hero save Allun's bread from burning, perhaps? Did the fearless Rin gardeners fight a plague of slugs with their bare hands? Who knows what terrors await us in this tale? I shudder to think of them."

The Traveler children shouted with laughter.

Annad jumped up. "Stop laughing!" she shrilled. "Our story is just as good as one of yours."

Rowan pulled at her dress. "Hush, Annad," he whispered. "Ogden is only teasing us." But as she sank back to the ground, he knew that his little sister was not the only one to be infuriated by Ogden's words.

Many of the Rin children, and the adults, too, were frowning. Already some of them distrusted the Travelers. And they did not like to be teased.

But Allun had not lost his smile. "You may mock, Ogden," he said in his light, clear voice. "But remember that the people of Rin were not always simple farmers. Our ancestors were warriors. Remember that in the past our two peoples have fought side by side to defeat the enemy that would invade our land."

"Yes!" growled a familiar voice. The crowd stirred. People turned to look at the white-haired woman leaning heavily on her cane in the shadows. Rowan's heart sank as he recognized old Lann.

"You were happy enough to stand behind our strength when the Zebak came, Traveler!" she called. "Remember their iron cages. Remember the War of the Plains. Remember our many dead. Remember these before you make jokes at our expense."

The Rin crowd muttered agreement.

"We remember, respected old one," said Ogden peacefully, holding out his hands to the fire. "We Travelers do not forget. We do not forget, for example, that your warriors depended on the Travelers' cunning and knowledge to make their plans and set their traps."

His voice dropped. "We do not forget how Travelers fed and sheltered them when they would have starved on the wild plains, far from their little fields and cozy homes and well-stocked storehouses. And we do not forget how Travelers fought beside them and died, too, in their hundreds, when they could have slipped away to safety and left them to perish alone."

He half smiled. "No," he murmured. "We forget nothing. Though others seem to—all too easily." He picked a slip-daisy leaf from the ground and looked at it thoughtfully.

There was silence around the campfire. An

uncomfortable silence. Then Ogden looked up. His eyes glinted, dancing like the flames, and his smile broadened.

"But still you speak truly, Lann of Rin," he purred. "Your short history is a history of heroes, as well we Travelers know. We know how highly you value courage."

His wide lips twitched. "You value it as highly as you value hard work, solid houses, full bellies, and settled ways. And that means you value it very highly indeed. We know this, though we do not pretend to understand it. And if sometimes we useless Slips mock, it is only because of our ignorance, people of Rin. We would sooner enter the Pit of Unrin than knowingly offend you. We beg that you will forgive us." He bowed his head.

Many of the Rin people nodded solemnly. But the Traveler children smothered giggles in the palms of their hands. Rowan knew that Ogden was making fun again. And he knew, too, that underneath the joke was something darker. Lann's words had cut into old wounds. They had cut deeply.

Allun felt it, too. Rowan could tell by the nervousness in his eyes and the tightness of his mouth. But he simply nodded to Ogden and smiled at the crowd. "Well, now that that is settled," he said, "may I tell my story?"

Ogden spread out his hands. "Tell on, Allun, son of Sara of Rin and Forley of the Travelers," he said coolly. "The blood of both our peoples runs in your veins. Our ears are open to your words."

"Tell well, Allun the baker," called old Lann. "But guard your rattling tongue. We want no long-winded ramblings. Take care you add nothing that is not needed to the tale."

Ogden raised his slanted eyebrows and shot a curious glance in her direction.

But Rowan knew her meaning. Lann feared that as part of his story Allun would tell how he had found sweet red berries growing by the Mountain caves. She feared that he would boast of how he had eaten some of them, given some to Marlie, and then filled his pockets with others, to bring them home to Rin. She feared he would tell their secret.

"Do not be alarmed, Lann," Allun said lightly. "I will not fail you."

He fixed his eyes on Ogden and raised his voice.

"One morning," he began, "the people of Rin woke to find that the stream that flowed down the Mountain and through their village had slowed to a trickle. By nightfall, even that small flow had stopped. . . ."

A hush fell over the crowd around the campfire. Rowan saw Traveler adults stopping to listen, moving closer. He recognized Zeel, the chief Forerunner, as she slipped into the circle. The Travelers knew that the stream meant life to Rin and to its bukshah herd. Even Ogden's eyes had lost their spark of mockery.

Rowan closed his eyes as Allun spoke on. He did not need to hear this story. He had lived it, with Strong Jonn of the Orchard, Allun the baker, Marlie the weaver, Bronden the furniture maker, and Val and Ellis from the mill.

Six months ago the seven of them had climbed the forbidden Mountain to find the source of their dried-up stream and try to bring its sweet water back to Rin. And in the end, as Sheba had foretold, it was Rowan, the smallest, weakest member of the party, who had succeeded in the quest.

But Rowan knew he wasn't a hero, really. Just as Sheba had said, he was still the same boy he had always been—shy and full of fears.

It was just that now he understood that there were different kinds of courage. He knew now that if those he loved needed help, he could feel terror, face it, and do what he had to do.

That knowledge warmed him. The cold, lonely feeling that had ached in his chest ever since his father died years ago had disappeared. He was happier now, by far, than he had been before he climbed the Mountain. As Sheba had said, it had taught him well.

But he did not *feel* like a hero. Not at all. And when people called him one, he was uncomfortable. He fidgeted now in his place on the grass. He wished with all his heart that he could slip away, find Jonn and his mother, and talk to them. But it was impossible. It would be seen as great discourtesy for him to leave the campfire now. He would have to wait.

Annad's small hand tugged at his shirt sleeve. "They are listening," she whispered. "Look at them. Wait till they hear what you did, Rowan. Wait till they know the dangers you faced to save the village."

She puffed out her chest. "I hope they know *I'm* your sister!" she added.

Her eyes darted around, watching the Traveler children as they crouched, wide-eyed, by the fire. "They will not dare make fun of us after this." She nodded with satisfaction.

Rowan patted the hand that clung to him. "I would not be too sure of that, Annad," he whispered back. "Travelers like to laugh. They take nothing seriously for long."

Allun's tale was ended. There was silence around the dying embers of the campfire. Then the Travelers and the people of Rin alike clapped and cheered.

Allun grinned at them and held out his hand to Rowan, crouched in the shadows. Rowan knew he wanted him to stand. But he could not do it. He shrank back, not wanting the curious eyes of the Travelers to find him.

"So!" said Ogden, stirring his fire thoughtfully. "So, Allun. Now I have another tale to tell through the land. The tale of Rowan of Rin."

He nodded. "It is a fine story," he said. "You told it well." Then he smiled. "But I will tell it better."

Everyone laughed, Allun loudest of all.

Ogden dropped the stick he was holding and leaned forward. "And now, Allun, we must talk, in private," he said.

Allun hesitated, and Ogden frowned slightly. "There are questions I must ask you." He paused. "The Mountain is a great mystery. It is said that the people of the Valley of Gold climbed it, before the

Giants of Inspray fought and hid them from our sight. But I have waited long to meet a witness who can tell me of its wonders. Please do not disappoint me, Allun."

A small silence fell on the group around the fire. Rowan could feel that the people of Rin were holding their breaths.

"I fear I must disappoint you, Ogden," said Allun. "I cannot stay. My mother is tired, and I need to return to the village with her."

"Then I will come with you," Ogden answered pleasantly. "The three of us will share a cup of soup in your warm kitchen, as we so often have before."

Again Allun hesitated. Rowan could almost feel the pain behind his smile. And pain was easy to see on Sara's face as she stood clutching her son's arm.

"We prefer, this season, that none of your tribe come to the village, Ogden of the Travelers." Lann had stepped forward. Her voice was firm and strong, and she looked Ogden straight in the eye. "We find that your visits excite the children. And they are tired after the long winter. We ask, therefore, that you respect our wishes and keep to your camp."

Not a muscle in Ogden's face moved. It was impossible to tell what he was thinking. But Rowan could see the darkening faces of Zeel and the other

Travelers around the fire. They were not taking this refusal well.

"Perhaps you could talk to another member of the Mountain party, Ogden," Sara broke in, desperate to make peace. "Strong Jonn of the Orchard is here. And Marlie the weaver, too."

Ogden stared at her for a moment. He seemed to be thinking.

"Another time I would very much like to speak with every one of the Seven," he said politely at last. "But for now . . ." His piercing eyes searched the faces around the campfire. "Let me meet the boy Rowan. He, in particular, is of interest to me."

Rowan shuffled his feet and felt his ears grow hot. He felt Annad pushing at him excitedly. He knew that he was going to have to stand and go forward to meet the man by the fire. But he did not want to do it. He did not want to do it at all.

He forced himself to his feet and stumbled forward. He felt the eyes of the crowd upon him. But the only eyes he saw were Ogden's: deep, dark, drawing him in.

8 ∽ THE STORYTELLER

"So, Rowan of the Bukshah," said Ogden, putting out a thin brown hand to beckon him closer. "We have much to talk about. This is the second time I have heard of you this day. You were on the hill with the Welcomers, I am told."

Rowan nodded. He remembered the curious looks the Forerunners had given him. So they had remembered his name and reported it to Ogden. Why? he wondered. Why had they been interested in a messenger boy?

Ogden put his head on one side. "You think and wonder much, do you not?" he said in a low voice. "More, perhaps, than most of your people. And perhaps you sometimes feel apart from them because of this. Perhaps you feel most quietly content tend-ing the great beasts you serve. Would that be so, Rowan of the Bukshah?"

Rowan stood motionless, not knowing what to do. Was this man able to see into his mind? Into his soul? He looked nervously behind him. Where were his mother and Annad? Where was Jonn?

He saw that they were standing watching a Traveler magician make a small silver bell appear and disappear. The magician's hands moved like fluttering birds, throwing the bell this way and that, so that it shone in the firelight, winking in and out of sight. Annad's mouth hung open in wonder.

"Do not fear me," said Ogden, still in that quiet, gentle voice. "I mean you no harm. I merely wish to ask you some questions. Simple questions. I wish to understand you better."

Rowan felt his cheeks grow even hotter. He made himself stand straighter, and prepared himself to meet whatever was coming. He knew it would be difficult to lie to this man, with his all-seeing eyes. Rowan did not know what he would do if Ogden the storyteller asked him directly if anyone had brought anything with them down from the Mountain.

But to his puzzlement and relief, Ogden did not. He asked instead about Rowan's mother and his father. He asked about the bukshah and the life

Rowan led. And at the end of the questioning he took the boy's chin in his hand and looked deep into his eyes.

"Honest as the day is long," he said, and dropped his hand. He glanced at Rowan's bewildered face, and his lips curved briefly.

"Your ordeal is ended, Rowan of the Bukshah." He sighed. "You are free to go, with my blessing."

Rowan ducked his head and carefully moved back from the fire. When he dared to glance up, Ogden had put his hands behind his head and was gazing up at the starry sky. His brow was deeply furrowed, as if the worries of the world had settled on his shoulders.

Rowan turned and scuttled away.

Soon afterward Rowan walked home with Annad, Jiller, and Strong Jonn. It was past Annad's usual bedtime, and she was sleepy. But she was still chattering about Allun's story as she trotted along, bubbling with pride and excitement.

Rowan looked at his mother, striding tall and strong beside him. Despite her anger over the decision to forbid the Travelers from entering the village, she looked livelier than she had for many days. The visit to the hills had done her good.

Should he tell her and Jonn about Sheba now? He did not really want to do it in front of Annad. Perhaps he should wait until they were home and Annad had gone to bed. A few minutes' more delay would not matter one way or another.

Besides, under this starry sky with his family around him, his fear was starting to seem childish. The more he thought about the scene under the trees, the less certain he was that Sheba had not been tricking and teasing him.

Jiller turned and saw him looking at her. "You did well, Rowan," she said quietly. "I watched you talking to Ogden the storyteller. You were calm and stood straight. I was proud of you."

Rowan said nothing. He still felt shaken after his time with Ogden. He was sure that the man's questions, which had seemed on the surface so simple, had had some meaning that he had not understood. But still his heart was warmed by his mother's words. She did not often say such things. She thought it better to teach him to be strong and not to look for praise for doing what he should.

"Rowan showed them." Annad yawned happily. "He showed those Slips a thing or two."

"Annad!" exclaimed Jiller, half shocked, half laughing. "Do not call the Travelers by that name."

Annad yawned again. "Why not?" she asked. "Everyone else does. Everyone calls them Slips."

"Everyone else does *not*, little one," Jonn put in firmly. "Your mother does not. I do not. Marlie and Allun do not. Only those who wish to insult the Travelers use the word."

"Oh." Annad thought about that. "Why?"

"Such people think the Travelers serve no useful purpose," Jiller explained. "So they call them Slips, after the wild slip-daisies."

"Why?" Annad asked again. Her eyes were nearly closing with weariness, but she stumbled on determinedly beside them. "Why?" she repeated.

Rowan saw Jiller and Jonn smile at each other over Annad's head.

Then Jonn swung the little girl up into his arms.

"Because the slip-daisies have no use or purpose," he told her as he strode along. "When our people first came to Rin, slip-daisies grew wild all over the valley, as they do still on the hills and beyond. But as useful crops were sown, and houses and lanes were built, the daisies were weeded out. Other plants, it seems, do not thrive where slip-daisies grow. So good farmers do not like them. As some do not like the Travelers."

Annad thought about this. "Slip-daisies are not

completely useless," she argued. "Their roots make the medicine that Sheba sells us, for Rowan's nose."

Jonn laughed. "Their pollen makes skinny rabbit's nose run, and then their roots make it stop," he said, glancing at Rowan. "The disease and the cure in one small plant. Truly nature is very strange and wonderful."

They reached Bree and Hanna's gardens, and Jonn stopped. Rowan sniffed. Even his blocked-up nose could sense the sweet scent of the Mountain berry flowers drifting deliciously on the cool air.

"I must leave you here," Jonn said, swinging Annad to the ground. "I am to stand guard with Bree and Hanna this night."

Rowan felt a stab of disappointment. He had been sure that Jonn would come home with them, to sit by the fire for a while. He had done it so often before! What bad luck that on the very night that Rowan needed him he was staying away.

Jiller pulled her shawl more tightly around her shoulders. "Watch well," she said. "I am afraid, as others are, that Allun will tell Ogden of the Mountain berries. He has not so far. And he and Sara left the gathering early tonight. But they may go back later, alone, and then who knows?"

"Allun is not a fool. He will keep his mouth shut, as will his mother," said Jonn firmly. "Why do you think they left the camp early? They want it to be clear to everyone that should the Travelers find out about the berries, it was not Allun or Sara who told them."

"Yet Allun is half Traveler himself," Jiller argued. "And he thinks the fuss about the Mountain berries is foolish."

"Mother!" protested Rowan, shocked by her words. "Allun would *never* betray us!"

Jiller said nothing.

"I thought you were his friend!" Rowan said accusingly.

"I am Allun's friend indeed, Rowan," Jiller said gravely. "But this does not mean that I cannot see his faults. I agree, he would never betray us knowingly. But he may not agree that telling of the Mountain berries would *be* betrayal."

She bit her lip. "Traveler blood runs strongly in Allun's veins. He believes that growing things belong to all. He cannot understand why the Rin people wish to keep his gift a secret. I know this, because he has told me. He has told Marlie, too."

Rowan started to speak again, but Jonn held up his hand to quiet him.

"Whatever Allun does or does not do, both he and I are fairly sure that the Travelers know of the new crop already, Jiller," he said. "And if they do not, they soon will."

"But how?" cried Jiller. "Lann told Ogden that—"

"Lann's insulting order will not stop the Travelers from visiting the village in the night, if they so choose," said Jonn quietly. "And then they will have only to use their eyes and noses to find the Mountain berry bushes. They are everywhere!"

Jiller sighed.

"I do not think we need to fear, Jiller," Jonn told her gently. "There will be Mountain berries in plenty in Rin next year. More than enough to ensure good trade, and feasting, too."

He smiled. "Soon the Mountain berries will be so many, they will be as thick as the slip-daisies used to be," he said. "People will start complaining about them, and calling them wild and useless, and pulling them out."

"I doubt that," Jiller laughed. "The flowers are beautiful. The scent is wondrous. And never have I tasted such sweet, rich berries. Good for eating, cooking, making into juice—"

"Will no one want my hoopberries then, when

the Mountain berries thrive?" Jonn asked, hanging his head and pretending to mourn. "Will my trees disappear from the valley like the slip-daisies have? Then I will have to trudge up to the hills, like Sheba does, to harvest my crop."

"That will never happen. I like hoopberries *much* better than Mountain berries," Rowan said stoutly.

"So do I," cried Annad. She loved the Mountain berry fruit. But she loved Jonn more.

Jonn stretched wearily. "Well, I must bid you all good-night and let you go to your warm fire." He yawned and began moving toward the garden gate.

"Ho!" Rowan heard him call, as he rattled the gate. "Hanna! Bree! Open!"

There was silence from the gardens.

"Bree! Hanna!" roared Jonn good-humoredly. "Are you deaf, or asleep? Let me in!"

Silence. Deep, dark silence.

Rowan shivered. Far away he could hear low, restless bellows from the bukshah fields. And from the hills, faint music.

There was an exasperated grunt and then a clattering sound as Jonn heaved himself up onto the locked gate and jumped down to the ground on the other side.

"What do you think you're playing at, you two?" Rowan heard him shout. "Where are you? If I find you're snoring in your bed while I—"

There was a gasp. A silence. Then there were the sounds of running feet and of the gate being unbolted from the inside. Jonn's voice came again, sharp and urgent.

"Rowan! Jiller! Come quickly!"

9 ∿ TROUBLE

They bent over the two shapes huddled facedown on the ground beside the Mountain berry garden. Stakes lay scattered on the grass around them.

"They are breathing!" exclaimed Jiller. "Oh, they are so still that at first I thought—"

"So did I," Jonn said grimly. "But they are alive, all right. And yet they will not wake."

He shook Bree's shoulder. The man did not stir. "You see?" he said.

"The children!" gasped Jiller. Without another word she sprang up and ran to the darkened house that stood nearby, behind some fruit trees.

Rowan waited nervously for her return. Bree and Hanna's three children were not particular friends of his. They were too scornful of his shyness and teased him too much for that. But he hated to think of them in danger, or crouching terrified in that dark house, with their parents lying so still outside.

In a moment Jiller had returned. "Sleeping, tucked up in their beds," she said. "They seem safe enough. But I did not try to wake them. For all I know they have the same illness as their parents."

She put her hand to Bree's cheek, gleaming white in the deep shadows. "He has no fever," she said. "But this is not a natural sleep, Jonn."

She looked around, shivering, as though on guard for watching eyes. "I feared something like this would happen," she said, putting her arm around Annad's shoulders. "I feared it as soon as I heard the children shouting this afternoon."

Quickly she glanced at the bushes in the garden beside them. "I do not know if they have been disturbed, or if any fruits are missing," she muttered. "I cannot tell in the darkness."

Jonn stared at her, his mouth tight. Then he shook his head as though to clear it. "We will talk of this later," he said. "Now we must tend to Bree and Hanna. We must move them to shelter, Jiller. They are heavy, but between us I think we can manage it."

"Do you want me to go for help?" asked Rowan. "Bronden's house is near. And Marlie's."

Jonn hesitated. "No," he said finally. "I think for now we would be better dealing with this on our own, Rowan. We do not want news of it to travel too quickly. Until we know . . ."

He looked straight into Rowan's eyes. "You understand?" he asked.

Rowan nodded. He knew as well as Jonn what would happen if rumor spread that Bree and Hanna had been struck down. He knew that some villagers would not hesitate to storm up to the Travelers' camp with lanterns and torches, to accuse and threaten.

And that would be dangerous. Dangerous to the whole of Rin.

It would be much better if Jonn and Jiller could wake Bree and Hanna and get the real story of what had happened to them. Something simple could be at the heart of this. Something that had nothing to do with the Travelers at all.

"You can help by staying here and keeping watch, skinny rabbit," Jonn said. "No task is more important now than keeping intruders from the gardens."

"I will help!" Annad insisted sleepily. "I will keep watch, too."

Jonn smiled at her, his teeth white in the dimness. "I am depending upon it, Annad," he told her.

"Call us if there is the faintest sound to alarm you, Rowan," warned Jiller.

Rowan nodded. He watched his mother and Strong Jonn bend to lift Bree's limp body, then begin to carry it toward the cottage that stood just beyond the gardens.

Jiller and Jonn, staggering slightly under their burden, disappeared into the shadows of the house. Left alone with Annad and the sleeping Hanna, Rowan strained his eyes in the darkness. Shafts of moonlight stretched in bands across the gardens.

It was quiet now. So quiet that Hanna's deep breaths sounded loud. There was no sound from the bukshah fields. No sound from the camp on the hill. And yet the silence was not peaceful. It was like the silence of waiting: heavy and full of secrets.

> The secret enemy is here.
> It hides in darkness, fools beware!

Rowan felt his sister's weight grow heavy on his shoulder. He looked down and saw that her eyes were closed.

"Annad," he said. "Do you want to go inside the house, to sleep there?"

She forced her heavy eyelids open. "I don't want to sleep," she murmured. "I am keeping watch."

"So you are," he agreed. "Watch, then."

She nodded happily. Her eyelids fluttered closed again.

Rowan put his arm around her to keep her warm. He watched, peering into the darkness beyond the gardens, searching the shadows for the tiniest, stealthiest movement. He listened, in the deep silence, for the slightest sound. He waited for the smallest sign that someone or something was lurking near, watching and listening as he was.

But there was nothing. Only a droning, chanting voice in his head. And to go with the voice, a picture. Sheba, with fear on her face.

He heard his mother and Jonn moving out of the house and toward the gardens. They were coming back for Hanna.

He glanced at Annad. She was sleeping heavily. She would not wake. He knew the time had come.

"Jonn, Mother," he whispered piercingly. "I have something I have to tell you. Now!"

Jiller's eyes were dark with fear.

"What does this mean?" she breathed. "What does it mean, 'the old wheel turns'?"

Rowan looked at her in surprise. He had not thought much about this part of the rhyme.

"I don't know," he said. "I don't know what *any* of it means. And neither does Sheba. But she is afraid."

They stared at him. A cloud glided over the moon, and the gardens darkened. A bird rustled in a nearby tree. Annad muttered in her sleep and stirred against Rowan's shoulder.

Jonn stood up. "We need help, I think," he said. "We cannot keep this matter a secret any longer."

Jiller nodded. "It is late. We cannot rouse the whole village at this hour."

"Nor do we want to," Jonn said grimly. "Rowan must go and wake only those who can be of real help."

"Timon," Rowan suggested. To him, Timon the teacher was the one most likely to be able to think clearly about Sheba's rhyme. And one of the villagers least likely to panic.

"Yes," Jiller agreed. "Timon. And Marlie."

"And Allun," added Jonn.

"I do not think it would be wise to bring Allun into this," Jiller said. "For plainly the Travelers have something to do with it."

"Then who better than Allun to help us?" asked

Jonn. "We are fortunate to have a friend who knows the Travelers' ways."

Jiller said nothing, but Rowan could see that she was troubled.

"I will go and get Timon, Marlie, and Allun, then," he broke in quickly.

It worried him to see Jonn and his mother disagree. There was a time when he had hated the idea that one day Strong Jonn of the Orchard might marry Jiller, and become his stepfather. But now he felt differently. Jonn would never take his father's place in his heart. But he had made his own place— the place of a good and special friend, to be depended on and loved in his own way.

"Yes, Rowan," Jiller said quietly. "And also bring Lann."

Rowan and Jonn stared at her in surprise. She returned their looks gravely.

"I have been thinking of the rhyme," she said. " 'The old wheel turns,' it says. And it talks of 'the same mistakes, the same old pride.' It seems to me that it is telling us that whatever trouble we are facing has been faced before."

Rowan's heart thudded. He had suddenly remembered what Sheba had said, before the chant began.

The enemy is coming again, she had said. *The wheel is turning. And this time—this time—*

He repeated the last lines of Sheba's chant aloud.

"For day by day its power grows,
And when at last its face it shows,
Then past and present tales will meet—
The evil circle is complete."

He shuddered. He knew his mother was right. Something dreadful was going to happen. And it had happened before. Slowly the wheel of time and fate was turning. Some evil circle was forming. And when it made a perfect whole . . .

Jiller looked at Jonn. "The answer to this lies in our past," she said. "I am sure of it."

He nodded slowly.

"Lann is the oldest person in the village," Jiller went on. "She remembers much that even the books do not tell us. If the trouble we face now has happened before, Lann will know of it. She may be able to help us stop it, before the wheel turns any further."

"You are right," exclaimed Jonn. He spun around to Rowan. "Go then," he ordered. "Go quickly."

10 ～ THE SECRET ENEMY

Timon stroked his chin. "The books tell us that hunger has always been an enemy for Rin to fear," he suggested. "We have faced it several times when crops have failed or the winter snows have cut the village off from the coast for too long."

"I doubt it is the enemy of the rhyme, though," said Jiller. "The rhyme says the enemy is here already. In hiding, perhaps, so we do not recognize it. But here."

"I believe we should go to Sheba," Marlie said. "We should ask her what the rhyme means."

"She does not know!" Rowan exclaimed. "I told you."

"She did not know when you spoke to her, Rowan,"

Jonn answered. "But by now her knowledge may have grown. We should try."

Lann nodded. "True enough," she said. She pointed her stick at Rowan. "The boy should go. And Jiller and Jonn with him. The rest of us will stay here with the sleepers. Timon will be company for me, Marlie can guard the Mountain berries. . . ."

"And I?" asked Allun with a twisted smile.

"I want you here under my eye, Allun the baker," said Lann calmly. "In case you decide to take a walk to the hills."

Allun's face darkened with anger, but he kept silent.

The orchard was dimly lit by moonlight. Rowan, Jonn, and Jiller did not speak as they moved through the hoopberry trees, treading carefully so as not to crush the sweet herbs and tender Mountain berry bushes that clustered underfoot. It was very quiet. No birds rustled in the trees. There was no sound from the bukshah fields.

They climbed through the fence that marked the end of the orchard and began walking quickly over the pale grass that grew in front of Sheba's hut.

The door stood open, and light streamed, flickering, from the room beyond. Light, and the long shadow of someone moving around inside. Rowan felt his heart begin to beat faster. He glanced at his mother. Her face was set and determined, but he could tell by her rapid breathing that she, too, was afraid.

They reached the door and looked inside. Sheba was there, bent over the great iron pot that hung above the glowing fire. She was muttering to herself, stirring the brew.

"Sheba!" Jiller said softly.

The old woman turned slowly. She stared blankly at Jiller and Jonn. And then she saw Rowan. Her glazed eyes widened, and she threw up her hands with a cry of fear, as if to protect herself.

"Leave me!" she gasped. "Leave me be! Take your nightmare face away!"

Rowan stepped back in shock.

"We need to talk to you, Sheba," said Jonn urgently. "The rhyme you gave to Rowan. What is its meaning?"

She shook her head, shutting her eyes. "Leave me," she moaned. "Leave me to do my work. There is no time. No time left."

The firelight leaped behind her. The evil-smelling brew in the cauldron bubbled.

"The work does not matter now," Jiller exclaimed.

"The rhyme is what matters, Sheba. You must tell us what you know."

"I know nothing," the old woman droned. "Nothing but my nightmares. And all of it—all—is coming true. I feel it. Even now the wheel is turning. And soon the enemy will be upon us. Soon, soon—"

"Sheba, help us!" Jonn begged.

But Sheba's face was empty. "I must make the brew. This I can do. This is what I know. The boy—take him away. His face haunts my dreams. The face . . . three kites . . . the golden owl with green eyes . . ."

Rowan heard his own strangled gasp and his mother's sharp cry.

"All of them—torment me!" Sheba thrust her fingers into her hair and swayed. "And I do not know why. I only know that I must work. I must go on. And I am tired, so tired. . . ."

She took a staggering step toward them. "Leave me, tormentor!" she screeched, looking directly at Rowan. *"Leave me!"*

Jiller put an arm around her son and held him tightly.

"Let us go," said Jonn. "There is nothing more for us here."

* * *

Old Lann hobbled to the partly open window. For a moment she stared out at the tall figure of Marlie still standing on guard by the Mountain berries. Then she turned to face the others.

"Three kites—what can this mean but the Travelers? And the golden owl with green eyes is a symbol of that Travelers' tale—the Valley of Gold. We must take good note of these visions. Sheba may not know what they mean. But they are warnings. Of that there is no doubt."

"She said the wheel was turning," said Jiller fearfully. "She said that soon the enemy would be upon us."

"But what enemy?" Timon frowned.

"Why look for secret meanings to the word?" Lann answered in a tired voice quite unlike her usual fierce tones. "Rin has only ever had one real enemy. The Zebak. We must arm ourselves and prepare for war."

There was silence in the cheery, well-lit living room. Rowan looked up at his mother. She had been to the bedroom to check on Bree and Hanna, still sleeping their strange, unnatural sleep.

She had returned just in time to hear Lann's words. Now she stood by the door, her hands pressed tightly together. Her eyes flickered to

Annad, curled up on the couch in the corner, then to Jonn, sitting at the big table, and finally to him.

She is afraid for us, thought Rowan. He watched her move swiftly to the table, and take her seat again. She looked exhausted. Gray shadows marked the skin underneath her eyes. Her face was pale.

"There has been no word of the Zebak coming again, Lann," she argued, leaning across the table. "No news from the Maris folk of strange ships near the coast, or rumor on the seas."

"It has been a long, hard winter, girl," said Lann. "No one from Rin has been to the coast since autumn. How do we know what is happening there? The Maris folk could be defeated and enslaved, even now."

"The Travelers would know," Timon put in. "And the Forerunners said they had no news."

"They said they had no news *to tell us*, Timon," Jonn corrected. "That is a different thing from having no news at all." He looked at Allun. "The Forerunners were keeping something back. I could feel it. It could be that the Travelers know something that they cannot or *will* not tell, for reasons of their own."

"Nonsense," said Allun, looking away.

Lann glared at him. "Is it?" she demanded.

Allun met her stern look with a calm one of his own. "Yes," he said quietly. "The Travelers would not keep news of a Zebak invasion from us. Not only because they are our friends, but because, as you pointed out at the camp this very night, Lann, because they *need* us."

"This is true, Lann." Jonn nodded. "The Travelers do not wish to be enslaved to the Zebak any more than we do. As Ogden told us this night, they well remember the War of the Plains. And they remember, too, the great battle before that, when our ancestors came to this place and were freed."

"Not just these, either," Timon's soft voice put in. "There are Travelers' tales of Zebak invasions going back for ages past. According to legend, their people were fighting a great battle against the Zebak on the coast at the same time as the Giants of Inspray were fighting on the Mountain for the Valley of Gold."

Lann scowled. "The Giants of Inspray—the Valley of Gold! Children's stories!"

Timon cleared his throat. "Perhaps," he said. "Fact and fantasy often mingle when a history is passed down only in pictures and the spoken word, as the

Travelers' history is. But it seems true enough that the Zebak have always wanted to take this land. They tried many, many times before we came here."

"And they always failed," Jiller reminded him.

"Yes," Timon agreed. "Their might has never been a match for the Maris folk's wits and the Travelers' knowledge of the land. In the end they were always forced back and driven away."

"And then they brought our race to these shores. And this was a fatal error," added Lann with satisfaction. "They thought to add to their strength with an army of warrior slaves. But instead the slaves rose up and turned against them, joining with those they wished to conquer. For the past three hundred years, instead of two peoples defending this land, there have been three."

She paused, and a shadow crossed her wrinkled face. "But we must consider whether there are three still, my friends. Or whether—as the witch's rhyme warns us—treachery is in the air."

"What do you mean?" cried Allun angrily.

Timon rubbed his hand across his tired eyes. "We must not let our feelings guide us, Allun," he said. "We must consider everything. What if—" He hesitated, glanced at Jonn and Jiller, and then went on.

"What if the Zebak, realizing they cannot win

this land by strength alone, have grown cunning? What if they have made promises to the Travelers— promises to give them something they dearly want, perhaps—in return for help?"

"The Travelers want for nothing. What could the Zebak promise them?" Allun demanded.

"Something they could get from no one else," Timon said simply. "The Zebak could promise to use their might to help the Travelers brave the Pit of Unrin and find the Valley of Gold."

11 ⌒ BETRAYAL

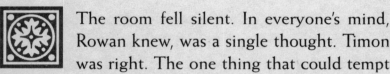The room fell silent. In everyone's mind, Rowan knew, was a single thought. Timon was right. The one thing that could tempt the Travelers was the chance to find the legendary place of all goodness that was at the heart of their tales. To rediscover, after thousands of years, the great, wise race of people who had been Traveler friends and allies.

"Think what it would mean to Ogden, to be the leader who gained for his people such happiness," said Timon. "The Pit of Unrin has always been a forbidden place to the Travelers. They cannot enter it, any more than they can climb the Mountain. If it is to be defeated, others must do the deed. And

Ogden knows that neither we nor the Maris folk would offer help to find the Valley."

"Why would we waste our time and endanger lives in such a quest?" Lann said at last. "The Valley of Gold is a legend. It does not exist."

"The Travelers believe it does." Allun's voice was flat and cold. "They believe it as they believe the sun rises in the east and sets in the west. They have no doubt." Suddenly he pushed back his chair and half stood. He was shaking his head violently.

"No!" he shouted. "No! The Travelers would never be taken in by Zebak promises! *Never!* Not even for this. Not even for the Valley of Gold. They are our friends. They would never betray us!"

Timon bowed his head. "The Zebak may at last have learned a lesson from the Travelers," he said. "They may have learned that you catch more bees with honey than with black looks and fighting words. They might, by trickery and lies, have turned the Travelers against us, Allun. Who knows?"

Rowan stared. *Beneath soft looks the evil burns.* He looked quickly at his mother and at Jonn. Had they realized how closely Timon's words matched the rhyme?

By their faces, he could see they had. And more.

They were remembering Sheba's visions. Three kites. The Travelers' kites. And a golden owl with green eyes.

He heard again Ogden's voice. "The Valley of Gold . . . houses painted with beautiful patterns, each one different . . . before each house, a golden bird—an owl with emerald eyes . . ."

Before he could say anything, there was a groan from the room beyond. Jiller sprang to her feet and ran to where Bree and Hanna lay. Everyone else quickly followed.

Bree was stirring, tossing his head on the pillow.

It was stuffy in the little room. Timon turned and threw open the window. The cool night air streamed in, bringing with it the scent of the Mountain berries and new grass, but no sound. No sound at all.

"Bree, what happened?" asked Lann sharply. "Tell us! Come on, man! Make an effort!"

Bree's eyes slowly opened. He gazed in bewilderment at all the people crowded into his small bedroom. Then he turned his head and saw his wife, still unconscious on the bed beside him.

"Hanna!" he groaned, and reached out for her.

"She is asleep, Bree, as you have been," Jiller told him. "Bree, we need to know what happened."

"We were building a fence," Bree mumbled. "Around the Mountain berry plants. To protect them from thieving Slips who may come in the night."

Allun made a sharp sound of disgust and protest. Jiller shook her head at him. She wanted Bree to go on.

"I was pounding stakes into the ground," said Bree. "Pounding them in, then sharpening the tips. But the ground was hard—like iron, it seemed. The stakes would not go in very far, however hard I hammered them. I got so tired. Then Hanna tried while I rested. But in the end she had to give up, too."

Rowan saw the adults around the bed look at one another over Bree's head. This was very strange. The soil in the gardens was rich and moist. Stakes should have entered it as easily as a knife enters soft butter.

"I was so tired." Bree sighed. "So tired. I had to lie down. To rest. So tired." His eyelids drooped. His mouth fell open.

"Bree!" cried Jonn, shaking him. But Bree did not answer. He was asleep again, and this time he would not wake.

"He is enchanted," growled Lann, angrily beating her stick on the ground. "He and Hanna, too. Not content with betraying us to our enemy, the Slips are after the Mountain berries. They hardened the ground to prevent the fence being built. They put the gardeners to sleep. And—"

"Perhaps they did put the gardeners to sleep!" hissed Allun. "But *if* they did—*if*, Lann, what of it? It is a harmless enough trick. It has nothing to do with the Zebak or Sheba's rhyme. You lurch from one thing to the next, you people, without thought, guided only by your dislike of the Travelers."

"That is not so, Allun." Jiller put her hand on his arm.

"It is!" he shouted, shaking it off.

"It is *not*," roared Lann, banging her stick. "Be still, Allun the baker!"

Jiller slipped quietly from the room. Rowan followed.

He found her bending over Annad, still lying on the couch. She straightened up to face him, her forehead creased with worry.

"I do not like this, Rowan," she said. "Already I feel the trouble coming upon us. We are arguing and fighting among ourselves when we should be banding together to face whatever is coming. Only that way can we be strong."

Rowan nodded. He felt close to despair. Sheba's words drifted into his mind.

The same mistakes, the same old pride,
The priceless armor cast aside.

Was this what the rhyme had meant? If so, then Sheba was right, and the evil circle was already nearing completion. The wheel was turning, every moment bringing the enemy closer and closer. He shuddered.

"Do you think Timon could be right?" Jiller murmured. "Could the Travelers have turned against us?"

"But why then would they have *come* here?" Rowan said.

"To spy!" said Lann from the bedroom door. Rowan watched her hobble to the fire. Her face looked withered and exhausted as she lowered herself painfully into an armchair.

"They have come here to spy on us," she said. "To report to their new friends on our food supplies and arms." Her head drooped, and she struggled to raise it. "I am tired," she mumbled. "So tired."

Jonn quickly crossed the room to kneel beside her.

The old warrior feebly waved him away. "The Slips have come to spy on us," she repeated.

Then Rowan saw her eyes widen. "Or something worse," she muttered.

She twisted in her chair to stare at them wildly. "Oh, we have been blind!" she shrieked. "Bree— Hanna—" She tried to get to her feet, but fell back with a groan.

"Lann, what is wrong?" cried Jiller in fear. She put her hand to her mouth and looked down at Annad, but her voice had not disturbed the little girl. She did not stir. A shadow of puzzlement passed over Jiller's face.

"Marlie," groaned Lann. "Quickly!"

Allun looked at her sharply and went to the door. He pulled it open and called to Marlie. But the tall figure standing in the garden did not turn or reply.

Jonn and Timon stepped forward, but Allun was already running. They heard his voice calling, more and more urgently in the silence of the night. "Marlie! Marlie! Answer me!"

"He will rouse the village," said Timon.

But nothing stirred. Least of all Marlie. For when, in answer to Allun's despairing cries, Rowan, Jonn, and the others rushed out to his side, they found him clutching and shaking her in terror, while she stood as still as a statue, her eyes fixed and staring.

* * *

"She breathes," Jiller said, bending over Marlie's rigid body lying by the fire. "But—"

"She will not wake," mumbled Lann. "One by one we are falling prey to this—this witchery. And this is the plan. We sleep—and then . . ." Her voice trailed off. She fell back in her chair.

It hides in darkness, fools beware!

With a cry Jiller jumped up and put a hand on the old woman's forehead. But she did not move. Jiller turned away, tight-lipped, and went to the couch where Annad lay.

"Why has no one come to find out what is happening here?" asked Timon suddenly. "Allun's shouts should have brought a dozen people running. Bronden's house is just nearby. And there are others. Many others."

"Perhaps they did not hear," said Jonn gravely. "Perhaps they are sleeping too deeply. Like Bree and Hanna's children. Like Bree and Hanna themselves. Like Marlie. And now, it seems, Lann."

Jiller made a small, anguished sound from her place on the couch. As they looked at her she licked her dry lips. "And Annad, Jonn," she whispered. "Annad—she—is like the others."

Rowan felt his stomach turn over. He ran over to

the couch and shook Annad violently. But the little girl did not move. He spun around to Allun, his eyes stinging.

"Allun!" he shrieked. "Allun, you have to tell the Travelers—to stop it!"

Allun stepped back. His face was white. "It cannot be," he said. "It cannot . . ."

Then he looked at Marlie on the floor, Lann slumped in her chair, Jiller crouched over the small bundle on the couch.

"I will go," he said softly. "And if this is my people's doing, I will have it stopped. I will, I swear it!" He gripped Jonn's arm. "Ring the bell in the square," he gabbled. "Ring it loud and long until some people come. We cannot be the only souls still in our senses this night."

"I will go," said Timon. "Jiller and Jonn can stay here with the sleepers, to see that no harm comes to them. You, Allun, go to the camp on the hill. Go quickly, and do not go alone. Take Rowan with you."

"No!" cried Jiller. "Why Rowan?"

"Ogden knows Rowan now, and respects him as the hero of the Mountain," said Timon. "He seemed to recognize something in the boy tonight. Something he found interesting, and that he liked. Next to Allun, Rowan is our best messenger."

"Yes," said Jonn. "Rowan should go. Sheba said she keeps seeing his face in her dreams. Perhaps he is to play his part in this mystery now."

Jiller nodded and slumped wearily back on the couch, with Annad's head on her lap. She looked exhausted. The gray smudges under her eyes had darkened to black.

"Mother! Don't go to sleep!" warned Rowan anxiously.

Allun pulled at his arm. "Come now," he said. "Let us hurry!"

They left the house and began running through the village. Already the first pale signs of dawn were streaking the sky. As they reached the trees where Rowan had met Sheba, they heard the bell begin its warning, clanging sound.

Rowan imagined Timon standing alone in the square, his long fingers grasping the bell rope, pulling it over and over again. His ears would be deafened by the bell. His eyes would be searching the darkness for people starting half-awake from their beds in answer to his call.

Rowan and Allun burst from the trees and began racing up the hill. Rowan ran with his head down, panting and gasping.

He heard Allun curse, felt him falter and slow.

"What is it?" He choked. "Allun?"

Allun stopped.

"Look," he said, and pointed.

The hill where the Travelers had camped was bare and empty. They had gone.

12 ∽ THE WHEEL TURNS

Allun bent to feel the ashes of Ogden's fire.

"Still warm," he said. "They moved out only a few hours ago."

"Why did they go?" exclaimed Rowan. "So silently, without saying good-bye?"

Allun's mouth tightened. "Perhaps they were hurt and angry because the village of their so-called friends had been forbidden to them."

Rowan looked at his lean face, outlined against the lightening sky. At this moment, with his hair ruffled and his dark eyes secret, Allun looked very little like a man of Rin and very much like a Traveler.

"Or perhaps," the man went on in a hard voice, "they left because they had done what they came to do. Perhaps old Lann is right."

Rowan caught his breath.

"We must go back to the village," Allun said abruptly. He started down the hill.

"Allun!" Rowan cried. "What are we going to do?"

"We are going to visit my mother, and yours," said Allun, quickening his pace. "We are going to get water and food. And then we are going to find the Travelers and get to the heart of this matter, for good or ill, before it is too late. If the Zebak are coming—"

"But Allun . . ." Rowan panted, struggling to keep up with him. "How . . . ? Where . . . ?"

Allun glanced at the boy beside him. His voice softened. "Rowan, do not ask questions. Save your breath. We must hurry."

The village was quiet as they entered it. The ringing of the bell had stopped. But Rowan's heart leaped with relief as he heard low voices coming from the square. People were awake and gathered there, then. And they were not shouting in fear and panic. They were talking quietly to one another.

"It's all right," he said to Allun eagerly. "People are there. Maybe Annad has woken, too—and Marlie and the others."

But Allun's face looked set and grave.

"Wait," he said.

They turned a corner and reached the square. Timon was still standing by the bell. A dozen people were gathered around him. Others were moving into the square from laneways all around. Still others were walking quietly away.

Rowan blinked at the scene before him. And in that blink, his hope vanished. The gathering was all wrong. He had been pleased that there were no shouts of panic. But there should have been much more noise than this!

There should have been far more movement, too. There should have been children running, excited by the unexpected call. There should have been people walking briskly around, wanting to hear the news, wanting to know why they had been so rudely wakened.

But there was none of that. There were no children in the gathering. And the adults who were there seemed to be wandering in a daze. Their faces were dreamy and their voices low. Some had not even troubled to pull a coat on over their nightclothes but trailed around in white gowns and shirts, shivering, barefoot and tousled, like ghosts.

They were awake, yet not awake. It was as though they had simply stirred in the middle of sleep and would at any moment turn to sleep again. Even as Rowan watched, he saw Neel the potter sigh and sink slowly to the ground. The paving stones must have been very cold, but he curled up on them as though they were his own soft mattress and closed his eyes.

Rowan clapped his hand over his mouth to stop himself from crying out.

Allun crossed the square in three strides and grabbed Timon's arm. The teacher slowly turned, and to his horror Rowan saw that his face, too, was blank and empty.

Allun shook his arm. "Timon!" he called. "Timon, wake! Ring the bell again!"

He caught at the bell rope himself and pulled at it furiously. The sound of the bell rang out, shockingly loud, in the square. The people turned to look, and blinked, then turned away again.

"Timon!" shouted Allun. Timon's face cleared for a moment. He licked his lips.

"It is too strong, Allun," he mumbled. "It is growing. I cannot fight it anymore. And the others . . ." He shook his head.

Allun spun around to face Rowan. "Come with me," he said. He began to push his way through the people milling in the square. They barely looked at him, or at Rowan. They just moved aside gently as he passed, like grass bending in the wind.

The bakery door was closed. Allun pushed it open and walked through the cool, dark kitchen to the back of the house. "Mother!" he cried sharply.

But there was no answer.

"Mother!" Allun called again. "Answer me!"

But still no sound disturbed the silence.

Rowan watched helplessly as Allun darted from room to room, shouting, banging doors. He saw that the back door was open and went outside. The neat back garden lay spread out before him, dim and sweetly perfumed. And there . . .

"Allun," he gasped.

Sara was lying back in an old wooden chair on the grass, an overturned cup by her limp, hanging hand.

Allun bent over her. He touched her with trembling hands. "She was here, drinking soup, when you came for me last night. She must have been overtaken after I left. She has been here ever since. In the dark and the cold. Her clothes are wet with dew."

He buried his face in his hands. "What is happening here?" He groaned. "By my life, Rowan, what is happening? How could the Travelers do this? To Sara, who loved them? Last night she was laughing with Ogden himself. And now . . ."

He gathered the limp body of his mother into his arms and staggered with her toward the house.

"Go to the kitchen and get bread and water," he shouted over his shoulder. "And quickly, Rowan. Quickly! We must get to Jonn and the others as soon as we can, and go for the Travelers. Before we, too, are overtaken and there is no one left standing in the whole of Rin. The sun is coming up. And the enemy—"

But Rowan was already hurrying to the bakery kitchen, stuffing rolls into a bag and filling a flask with water from the great jug that stood beside the door. In a moment he was back at Allun's side. He watched as Allun covered his mother with a rug and leaned over her, fumbling with something at the back of her neck.

"Allun, come on!" he urged.

Allun straightened, pushed his hand deep into his pocket, and nodded. With a shock Rowan saw the paleness of his face, his hollow eyes.

"Allun!" he cried in fear. "You—"

Allun nodded. "I feel it," he murmured. "It is—a heaviness. Growing. I—"

Rowan tugged at his arm. "Come quickly," he said. "Come to the gardens. Do not stand still. Perhaps it is our movement that is keeping the illness from us. Come!"

He tugged Allun out of the living room and through the kitchen to the front door. Then he pushed him out into the street and took his hand.

"Run!" he whispered. "Run, Allun!"

They ran. Rowan could hear Allun gasping by his side. All around them in the street people lay sleeping on the hard stones. And now that it was lighter, Rowan could see that there were others.

Some were slumped in chairs in their gardens, like Sara had been. Some were lying by wells, with overturned buckets by their sides. Solla the sweets maker hung half in, half out of his window. A group of children who had been chattering around Ogden's fire only hours before were sprawled together under the Teaching Tree, still in the clothes they had worn to the storytelling.

Rowan pulled Allun through the square. They had to step over the bodies of people who lay there.

Timon stood by the bell, his hand still on the rope, his eyes unseeing. Rowan called to him, but not a flicker crossed the teacher's face.

They began to run for the gardens. And it was then that Rowan noticed the birds.

Birds of every kind lay scattered under the trees beside the path. Like small bundles of feathers they lay motionless among the Mountain berry flowers and the grass, as if they had fallen from their nests and perches in the night. Their eyes were closed. Their beaks gaped. Their legs were like tiny, stiff twigs.

Rowan's throat ached. It was as though every living thing in Rin had been captured by the spell that had overtaken the village.

"Star!" he whispered. His stomach lurched as he realized that the great beast must have known some trouble was coming. That was why she had been restless. That was why she had led the other bukshah away.

And he had made her return! If only he had seen that she would not have strayed without a cause. She had obeyed him at last, trusting him. But in his blindness he had made her bring her herd back into danger.

Sobbing, he pulled Allun on. They reached Bronden's workshop. Almost Rowan stopped, thinking to find help. But then he saw Bronden's stocky body, crumpled against her own front door. Her brow was creased, and her strong arms were flung out as though she had fought to the last against whatever power was clouding her brain and forcing her eyes closed.

"Rowan," mumbled Allun, dragging on his hand. "I cannot—"

"Yes, you can!" cried Rowan, panic-stricken. "Allun, look, Bree and Hanna's house is near. Do not stop. We have to find Jonn and Mother. They will help us."

He pushed through the gate that led into the gardens. He pulled Allun, stumbling, to the house behind the trees. And then he knew that there was no help to be found here either. For the door hung open, and Jonn lay facedown on the grass at the bottom of the steps, with Jiller at his side. They were still as death.

13 ∾ THE CALL

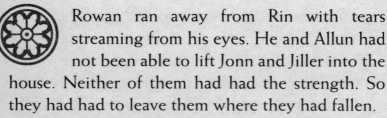Rowan ran away from Rin with tears streaming from his eyes. He and Allun had not been able to lift Jonn and Jiller into the house. Neither of them had had the strength. So they had had to leave them where they had fallen.

Never had Rowan done such a difficult thing. None of the horrors he had ever faced had matched that of turning his back on his mother lying helpless on the grass and running away.

Now he stumbled forward, his heart as cold and empty as a grate in which the fire had burned out. He barely saw the ground under his feet. He barely felt the dawn breeze against his face.

At the top of the hill he paused and looked down into the valley. Only yesterday he had done this, he thought. Then he had looked at those patchwork fields, and those tidy lanes and houses, and his heart had been warm. But that was before he had met Sheba under the trees. That was when the village had been full of life.

Without surprise he saw that the bukshah fields were still. He could see the bodies of some of the calves lying in the grass. But farther on—he bit back a gasp of relief—far away along the stream, other beasts were moving. And ahead of them all was Star.

In the night she must have decided to move the herd on after all. And she had done it. She, at least, had not made the old mistake. The mistake of trusting someone who did not know how wise she was to fear.

"Rowan," murmured Allun by his side. "Rowan, we must go on. This—this thing—you are right—grows more strong when I am still."

Rowan nodded and turned his back on the village. The thought crossed his mind that he might never see it again, and he shook his head. He would not think of that. He began walking.

The daisies under his feet were already doing their work. His eyes were puffing up, and his nose was running. Stop it! he told himself. He dug in his pocket for the hated medicine and took a sip. The disgusting, sour taste burned on his tongue. The memory of Sheba's cackle filled his mind.

But Sheba, perhaps, was not cackling now. Was she, too, hunched by her fire in a sleeplike trance, while the evil she had so feared made ready to show its face?

> *Then past and present tales will meet—*
> *The evil circle is complete.*

With a sinking heart Rowan faced the only possible meaning of those words. In the past, in a land far away, the people of Rin had been slaves to the Zebak. Now, after three hundred years of trying, the Zebak were about to swoop on them again. They were going to take them back into slavery. The evil circle would be complete.

And it would be soon. Very soon. Unless . . .

Rowan dug his fingernails into his palms. Unless he and Allun could find the Travelers, beg them to undo the mischief they had done, and stop the wheel from turning.

They moved on in silence. Rowan's legs were already tired, and he had been up all night. But his brain was working feverishly. They were following the tracks of the Travelers' carts. But the tribe had passed this way hours ago, and already the grass and slip-daisies were springing back into shape, softening their traces.

Soon they would disappear altogether. Then what would he and Allun do? And even if they *could* go on following the tracks, how could they possibly catch up, walking at this speed?

He looked up at Allun. The man's lean face was set, but his eyes were clearer now than they had been.

"You feel better, Allun," he ventured.

Allun nodded. "The movement helps," he said. "And you?"

"I never felt the tiredness," Rowan said. The thought had been troubling him. "I cannot understand it. Everyone else in Rin—even Bronden, even Jonn—was struck down. You are half Traveler, so it makes sense that you might escape. But why me?"

Allun shook his head. "Ogden took a fancy to you," he said lightly. "Perhaps he decided that you should be spared the sleep—and whatever evil is to follow it."

Rowan stared at him in horror. Somehow, despite everything, part of him had never quite believed that the Travelers had lulled Rin to sleep for a truly evil purpose. He had, he realized, clung to the hope that they had simply enchanted the village as a lesson. A strong lesson, perhaps, but a lesson that could be delivered, understood, and then undone.

But Allun's words filled him with dread. He bit his lip to stop himself from crying out and stumbled on.

Then Allun stopped, looked behind him, and dug in his pocket.

"We are far enough away now, I think," he said. "Now, Rowan. We will see what we will see."

He held out his hand. Cupped in it was a long, thin ribbon of faded, plaited silk. Sara's wedding necklace. Rowan had seen it a thousand times, around her neck. But he had never before noticed the small brown object that hung from it. It had always been hidden under Sara's clothes, he supposed.

He watched in amazement as Allun raised the tiny thing to his lips and blew.

No sound reached Rowan's ears. But he knew at once what was happening. The object was a reed pipe. Allun was signaling. He was calling the Travelers.

"I did not know Sara had a reed pipe," he whispered.

Allun brought the pipe down from his lips. "It has been a secret, until now. Mother was given it when she left the Travelers many years ago. She was told that she had only to call in time of trouble, and they would come. From anywhere. At any time. But it has never been used till this day."

"And *will* they come?" asked Rowan. "Even . . . ?"

Allun knew what he was thinking. Even though Sara's trouble was *caused* by the Travelers themselves?

"It was a solemn promise," Allun said gravely. "And if they fail to keep it . . ."

Rowan scanned the horizon, slowly turning to look in all directions. To the east and to the north, pale blue morning sky shimmered over hills golden with flowers. Behind them, to the west, the great Mountain rose, white tipped. Beside it, a little to the south, brooded the jagged rocks and caverns of—

He exclaimed, and pointed.

Three spots of color dipped and swayed against gray-brown distance. Moving closer.

"The Forerunners!" Allun breathed. Rowan saw him close his eyes for a moment, as if giving thanks. "They have heard me. They are coming."

The Forerunners slowed, skimmed the grass, lightly came to earth.

"Greetings, Allun, son of Forley of the Travelers," said Zeel. "Greetings, Rowan of the Bukshah." She walked forward, folding her kite behind her with one hand. The two boys stayed where they had landed. Watching.

"Greetings," said Allun after a moment. "We thank you for hearing our call."

"Where is Sara? Why have you summoned us?" Zeel asked.

"Sara is ill. I must speak with Ogden," Allun replied.

The Forerunner shook her head. "Ogden is with the tribe," she said coldly. "He cannot come."

Allun stepped forward. "I must speak with him, Zeel," he insisted. "I claim my right to a hearing. By my Traveler blood. By my father's name. And by ancient treaty." He bent and snatched up a slip-daisy leaf, holding it out to her.

Zeel regarded him suspiciously. Then she took the small three-lobed leaf from his hand, raised her pipe to her lips, and blew. She waited. A moment later she frowned and shook back her tangled curls. She had sent a message, and received one, Rowan thought in wonder. And he had heard nothing. Nothing at all.

"Ogden will grant a meeting," the girl said unwillingly. "But he cannot come to you. Will you journey to him?"

"How long will it take?" Rowan burst out.

"Not long," Zeel said. Her eyes were pale and cold. "You will fly, with the Forerunners. The Travelers will call the wind." She turned and walked back to where her friends were waiting, already spreading out their kites.

Rowan and Allun stared after her. She looked back. "Come!" she ordered. "Already the wind is changing. It is time to go. Ogden waits for you."

She paused, and over her smooth, suntanned face crept a shadow. A shadow of dread. "He waits," she said, "by the Pit of Unrin."

14 ~ SHOCKS

The wind flowed past Rowan's ears, and tugged at his hair. The strong leather belt that bound him to Zeel and her white kite cut into his ribs. Below him the ground slipped away. Fast. So fast. In moments they were far away from the hillside where they had met the Forerunners. In minutes the gray-brown distance was rushing to meet them.

So this was what it was to fly, to soar, like a bird on the wind. Rowan could not take it in. He was dizzy with a hundred different thoughts. His mother. Annad. Sheba. The Zebak. The Travelers. Ogden. Secrets. The Valley of Gold. The Pit of Unrin . . .

Around and around his mind raced while the kite sped on. The Pit of Unrin was not a legend. Not just a tale. It was a real place. And Ogden had taken the Travelers there. Why? Except that Timon's idea was right. The Zebak had promised the Travelers safe passage through the evil place and entry to the Valley of Gold.

Were the Zebak even now camped with their new friends? Were their savage faces, which Rowan had seen so often in books, showing false smiles as they whispered lies in Ogden's ear?

Were he and Allun flying with the wind into terrible danger? So they would die, and the last hope of help for Rin would disappear?

The Pit of Unrin. A legend of darkness, to balance the legend of light that was the Valley of Gold. Or so Rowan had always thought.

He had heard of it, often, in Ogden's tales. He could hear Ogden's low voice in his mind even now, whispering while the fire crackled and the children listened. ". . . And guarding the Valley of Gold, the hideous Pit of Unrin. It is a place of evil and darkness, a place of death. It is a place to fear. A place to dread. Hope, children, that you never, never see it."

The first time Rowan had heard of the Pit of Unrin, he had woken in the night, screaming with nightmares. That was when he was little and his father was alive. His father had come into the room, bringing with him the smell of soap, and clean towels, and the warm fire. He had gathered Rowan up in a hug, listened to his frightened babblings, smoothed his pillow, and laid him down again.

"Do not fear, small Rowan," he had said gently. "There is no such thing as the Pit of Unrin. It is only a story."

"But what if it is true?" Rowan remembered crying. "What if it is? And what if one day I have to go there?"

His father had smiled. "You will never have to go there, Rowan," he had said. "I promise."

He had thought he was speaking the truth. How was he to know otherwise? For the hardworking people of Rin never wasted time journeying to the barren lands beyond the Mountain. When they traveled, they traveled east, to the coast, to trade. The west was a mystery to them. A mystery they rarely wondered about and never tried to solve.

You could not know I would come here at last, Father, Rowan thought now, peering fearfully down as the kite began to glide lower and lower. No one could know. For even without the terrifying vision of the Pit of Unrin, why would anyone journey to this barren place?

The hard earth, softened only by a few scrubby

bushes, a sprinkling of slip-daisies, and tufts of spiky grass, rose up to meet his dangling feet.

He saw the tents of the Travelers pitched ahead, in the shadow of the Mountain, and the people themselves gathered together, watching silently. He saw the figure of Ogden standing alone near a steep hillock of cruel-looking rocks.

Were the Zebak there also? Rowan searched the ground desperately, looking for a sign. No. There were no helmeted figures, no weapons, no great machines of war. Were the Zebak hiding some- where near? Or were they even now marching into Rin, while the Travelers waited here to collect their reward for treachery?

There was no room in his mind for fear as his feet touched ground with a dragging thud that jarred his teeth and sent pains shooting up his legs. Suddenly he felt numb.

What was awaiting him in this terrible place?

He stood still as Zeel unbuckled the strap that had held him to the kite. He became aware that he was shuddering all over. He felt Allun's hand on his shoulder, and his knees nearly gave way.

"Allun—" He choked.

"Wait," said Allun, his face pale.

Zeel left them and went forward to Ogden. She handed him something. It was the slip-daisy leaf that Allun had given her.

Ogden took the leaf and raised his head to look at Allun. Then, slowly, he walked toward them.

"Greetings, Allun, son of Forley of the Travelers," he said. "What do you want of me?"

"I will not waste words, Ogden," replied Allun. "Time may be very short."

Ogden raised his slanted eyebrows. His dark eyes were unreadable. "Explain," he commanded.

Allun stared pointedly at the three-lobed leaf in Ogden's hand.

"Our peoples have been allies for three hundred years," he said. "For three hundred years our fortunes have been linked, so that we have been separate, but one."

Ogden said nothing. He rolled the stalk of the slip-daisy leaf around and around in his thin brown fingers.

Allun took a deep breath. "In the name of that old friendship, Ogden of the Travelers, I ask you to release the people of Rin from the curse you have placed on them," he said. "If we have been at fault, then we beg your forgiveness. We will do what we can to—"

"Wait!" Ogden ordered loudly, holding up his hand. His eyes flashed. Zeel and the other Forerunners ran to his side.

Allun had drawn back and was standing rigidly silent. Rowan moved closer to him and held on to his arm. His heart was thudding. Never had he seen Ogden, the mysterious, smiling storyteller, look like this. Frowning, fierce, and very angry.

"What do you mean by talking of curses to me?" Ogden demanded. "What lies are you trying to tell? What plans are you hatching? And by whose orders?"

Allun gaped at him in shock. He tried to speak, but no words came.

The same mistakes, the same old pride,
The priceless armor cast aside.

"We aren't telling lies!" Rowan burst out. He knew it was not his place to speak. But he could not bear to stand helplessly by while fear and anger got in the way of help for his home.

Ogden's black eyes turned on him. Rowan forced himself to speak on.

"Everyone in Rin is—is ill, because of what you did," he stammered. "Allun and I got away—to find you. To ask you to stop it." The hot tears stung in his eyes. He struggled to hold them back, but they spilled over and started rolling down his cheeks.

"The bukshah knew there was danger." He was sobbing as he spoke. "They heard your pipes—they must have understood what you were planning. Star tried to tell me, but I wouldn't listen. She took the herd away, away from the village and out along the stream. She kept them safe, all but a few little calves. But the people—my mother, my sister . . . they're lying helpless. And when the Zebak come—"

His throat closed up. He could hardly breathe. "Oh, please, please help them," he begged. "Don't make the rhyme come true. Don't!"

Ogden's face had changed. Now, mixed with the fierceness, there was bewilderment. He glanced at the three Forerunners by his side.

The two boys looked uncertain. But Zeel frowned and shook her head.

"It is a trick," she said. "Do not listen to the boy. They are using him because they know you liked him when you met last night. As they are using the other because he has the reed pipe and is half Traveler."

Her voice rose. "Why should these two be the only ones to escape this so-called illness? Why, except that there *is* no illness, and they have been chosen to track us down?"

"That is not true!" Rowan exclaimed, looking wildly at Allun and back to Ogden. What was happening here? The Travelers seemed to think that the people of Rin were the betrayers.

Ogden said nothing.

"It was a grave mistake to answer the call," Zeel cried passionately. "The enemy doubtless tracked our kites. And you are letting these spies delay our escape. As they hoped. We are wasting precious minutes. Let us go! Into the Pit of Unrin and on to the Valley of Gold, as we planned. It is our only chance!"

Rowan's stomach turned over. He looked closely at Zeel, the adopted daughter of Ogden the Traveler. He looked at her strong, straight black brows and her pale eyes. He looked at her height and her broad shoulders. Now that she was angry it was as though a mask had dropped from her face.

Take away the feathers, the flowers, the long hair, the bare brown feet, the loose, bright silk. Put on close-fitting clothes of steel gray, hard boots, a black streak from hair to nose, and Zeel would be a picture from the House of Books. A picture of a Zebak.

He pointed at her. "It is you!" he said. "*You* are the enemy! *You* are the spy! You have whispered poison to the Travelers and betrayed us all. You have done this to us! You!"

15 ∽ DARKNESS AND LIGHT

He leaped at Zeel, catching a glimpse of her startled face as he sprang forward. He beat at her with his fists. She stood unresisting, making no move to defend herself.

It was Ogden's hands that caught at him and pulled him back. Ogden's voice that commanded him to be still.

He struggled against the grip that held him, panting and choking still with the anger that had swept over him. His ears roared, and at first he could hardly hear what Ogden was saying to him.

"You are wrong, Rowan," Ogden was shouting. "Listen to me! Listen!"

Rowan finally quieted. Gradually his rage died in

him. He stopped struggling and stood shuddering under Ogden's hands.

"That is better," said Ogden. He glanced at Allun, and for the first time, his face was open.

"This child of Rin is far more fierce than he looks," he said, smiling faintly. "I see now why he conquered the Mountain."

"He is right to be fierce," Allun murmured, without returning the smile. "I have been blind. The Forerunner Zeel is a Zebak. And you must know it."

"There is nothing about my tribe I do not know," Ogden said quietly. "Zeel was a foundling, washed up by the sea, on the coast. We took her with us. She was born a Zebak, that is true. We knew it from her earliest days, though we did not speak of it to others. We feared they would react in the same way as our young friend Rowan has just done."

He squeezed Rowan's shoulders. His voice was sad.

Rowan looked at Zeel. She returned his look proudly, yet he could see the hurt in her eyes. He struggled to stay suspicious and angry. But he could not.

"Zeel was born a Zebak, but she has been raised a Traveler, from babyhood," Ogden went on. "She is one of us. She would die for us. If we have an enemy, it is not Zeel. Be assured of this. Zeel has said nothing to me that she did not truly believe. And she has said nothing that I did not fear myself."

He pressed his lips together. "Be assured of this also, people of Rin. The Travelers have done nothing to harm your friends."

"Why then did you come to us unexpectedly, and then leave so quickly, without warning?" asked Allun.

"We came because we felt a wrongness in the land," said Ogden simply. "We felt a danger. We came to you, as friends, to see if the trouble lay with you. And when we had come, we felt hardness. We felt secrets, and anger, under the smiling faces. We were forbidden the village and ordered to keep to the hills."

"But that was just because of the Mountain berries!" Rowan exclaimed.

Ogden paused. "The new *fruit?*" he said. "But why should that cause your people to close their hearts to us?" He frowned. "Rowan of the Bukshah, I fear you are mistaken. There must be something you do not know. Something far more—"

Allun was shaking his head. "No, Ogden." He sighed. "There is nothing else. The people of Rin—

it is hard to understand, I know—but they wanted to keep the fruit a secret. So as to breed a great crop that would be theirs alone, to sell on the coast next year."

Ogden stared in amazement. "But there was no secret, Allun," he said. "We knew about the new crop when we were still a day's journey away from Rin. We smelled its scent. We saw the stains of its fruit upon the birds. And why would anyone want to keep a source of food secret, just for gain? Are you *sure* . . . ?"

"Quite sure," said Allun firmly. "If you sensed secrets and suspicion in the people of Rin, that was the cause, Ogden. There is no other."

Ogden glanced at the three Forerunners, who were looking even more surprised and disbelieving than he was.

"It is incredible," he muttered. "I will never understand your mother's people, Allun. Never as long as I live."

He spread out his hands. "We thought you must have made an alliance with the Zebak against us. We decided to move on, to escape their coming. And it came to me that we should journey here. The place called me. And when the land calls, I listen."

He looked around him at the dry, rocky land. "I did not know the reason. But the Valley of Gold has been much in my thoughts of late. Visions of it keep rising in my mind unbidden. I thought perhaps I was drawn here because it was time at last for the Travelers to find again their ancient friends. They, then, could join us to fight the enemy, since you had deserted us."

"You think to find the people of the Valley of Gold?" whispered Rowan. "But is the Valley of Gold really true? I thought—"

Ogden smiled. "You thought it was but a legend? You of all people, Rowan of the Bukshah! Surely you know by now that all legends are silken threads woven around a gem of truth. And the Pit of Unrin is real enough." His face darkened, and he glanced behind him.

Rowan looked, but could see nothing but the jagged pile of rocks he had noticed before, and far beyond, a golden cliff face rising steeply toward the sky.

"The Pit of Unrin lies there, behind the stony hill," Ogden said. "And our tales tell us that it guards the Valley of Gold. This we believe. This we have always believed. Forerunners have flown across the Pit many times. But nothing can be seen from the air. Therefore we must enter the place of evil, to discover the secret way to our goal."

"But the Pit of Unrin is forbidden." Allun said. "Travelers cannot go there. It is their law."

Ogden nodded, his face grim. "Travelers born cannot. But—" He glanced at Zeel. "Zebak may do as they please. It has come to me that perhaps this is why Zeel was given to us. Perhaps it was always intended that she—and we—should finally come to this moment."

Zeel lifted her chin proudly.

Rowan struggled to put his thoughts into words. "But does all this mean that you—that the Travelers—did *not* enchant the village?"

"Of course we did not!" snapped Zeel, looking like a true Zebak again in her irritation. "Ogden has told you!"

Rowan felt himself blushing but made himself go on.

"Then how has it happened?" he pleaded. "And why?"

Ogden rubbed his thin hand over his mouth. "I do not understand," he said. Then his eyes narrowed. "You spoke of a rhyme," he went on. "What rhyme is this?"

"Our Wise Woman, Sheba, told it to Rowan the

day you came to Rin," Allun explained. "It was one of the reasons I—we—thought that you had betrayed us to the Zebak. It—fitted."

Ogden scowled. "Did it indeed? Well, perhaps you had better let me hear it, since it has done us such harm."

Rowan felt his face growing hot again. But he did as he was told, and spoke the words that he had grown to dread:

> "Beneath soft looks the evil burns,
> And slowly round the old wheel turns.
> The same mistakes, the same old pride,
> The priceless armor cast aside.
> The secret enemy is here.
> It hides in darkness, fools beware!
> For day by day its power grows,
> And when at last its face it shows,
> Then past and present tales will meet—
> The evil circle is complete. . . ."

Rowan's voice died away. Ogden was silent for a moment. Then he turned to Allun.

"I see why you were deceived," he said. He paused. "It is a puzzle," he went on. "And from it I draw one thing only. The answer to this trouble lies somewhere in the past."

"That is what my mother thought," Rowan broke in. "And Lann said the rhyme spoke of our enslavement to the Zebak and warned that it was going to happen again if we forgot old lessons."

Ogden nodded. "It could have been that," he said, "but I think that it is not. Both our peoples fear the Zebak. But perhaps there is another enemy for us both to fear."

"But how can that be?" cried Rowan. "We have known no other enemy since we came to Rin."

Ogden regarded him thoughtfully. "Ah, yes," he said. "But what of secret enemies, here before you came and after, but never revealed to you, or even to us, until now? Ancient enemies of the land and its people. Enemies who can wait a thousand years, two thousand, ten thousand, for the chance to strike again. What of those?"

He bent his head and closed his eyes. They waited. Rowan held his breath. Zeel's face was so still that it looked as though it was a molded mask.

Finally Ogden looked up. "I have thought," he said. "I followed my heart in coming here to this place, where it is said the Giants of Inspray fought and a wondrous valley was lost. I was called here, and the feeling is still strong in me. I cannot deny it. I know that here lies the answer that we seek."

He turned to Zeel. "Make ready, Forerunner," he said gravely. "You are, after all, to have your wish. You will go to seek the Valley of Gold. Are you still willing?"

She nodded, her face paling.

"The Pit of Unrin guards it," Ogden went on. "And the Pit of Unrin is a place of evil. Are you still willing?"

"Yes," she said in a low voice.

Ogden stared at the slip-daisy leaf, twirling it in his hand.

"You are Zebak born, and brave to your bones, my adopted daughter, Zeel," he said. "You are a Travelers' Forerunner, bred to face the unknown to protect and lead the tribe. But—" He glanced up at the two boy Forerunners, standing motionless beside him. "But on this journey Tor and Mithren, your usual companions, cannot go with you."

"I understand," said Zeel.

"Yet I am unwilling for you to face this evil alone. So I choose another to go with you. One whose help will prove that the old friendship between our two peoples is indeed unshaken. One who also follows his heart, and who has proved that he can face fear and danger in the quest."

He turned, and handed the leaf to Rowan.

16 ∽ THE NIGHTMARE

They climbed the hill of rocks without speaking. When they reached the top, Zeel embraced Tor, Mithren, and Ogden.

"I will see you again," she said to each of them in turn. And they repeated the words, looking into her eyes.

Allun gripped Rowan's hands. "Take care," he said. Then he caught Rowan in his arms and hugged him. "Take care," he repeated.

"Go now," said Ogden softly. "Listen to your hearts. They will guide you. We will await your call that all is well."

Rowan and Zeel turned and began to pick their way downward to the valley floor.

Rowan looked down, and his head began to

swim. Not because the drop was very steep, or the way too hard. Behind the hill of rocks the land sloped away quite gently, and tufts of grass and slip-daisies softened the ground underfoot.

His dizziness was caused by fear. Terrible fear. Because at the foot of the slope crouched a place that he would have known was evil even if he had never heard its name spoken. The very sight of it chilled him to the heart.

He could see only a mass of short, stubby trees. But they were hideous, not beautiful. Thick black trunks writhed up from the gray, dead-looking ground in a twisted mass. Dull purple-colored leaves clumped at the tips of the branches.

Here and there puddles of yellow fog crawled and clung around their roots. And there was a vile smell, like nothing he had ever smelled in his life. It filled his nose and clung to his clothes, making him sick with disgust and terror.

He looked across at Zeel, determinedly scrambling down the slope beside him. Her feet, covered now with soft shoes, did not skid on the loose, pebbly ground the way his did. The grass and daisies seemed to welcome her tread and cushion her every step.

She did not speak to him. She did not smile. She

had not wanted his company. She had wanted to go on this great adventure alone.

And Allun had not wanted Rowan to go, either. "Rowan is just a boy, Ogden," he had objected. "Surely I would do as well. I, too, am a citizen of Rin. If I accompany Zeel in Rowan's place, that will surely prove to you that the friendship between our peoples is as strong as ever."

But Ogden had shaken his head.

"Rowan of the Bukshah is almost the same age as Zeel, Allun," he said. "And Rowan was the only one of you to conquer the Mountain. I have great trust in him and his feeling for the land. And I feel a rightness in my choice. It is he I want to accompany Zeel."

Rowan slithered on the loose ground, trying to stay on his feet, knowing that Ogden and Allun and the two other Forerunners, Tor and Mithren, were watching him.

He felt his breath coming faster as the twisted trees of Unrin loomed larger and larger and the foul smell of the place rose up to meet him. He skidded the last few feet to the bottom of the slope and wished with all his heart that Zeel would talk to him. Say *something*. Just to keep his mind from his fear.

As if she had heard his thoughts, she turned to him. "Are you afraid?" she asked coldly.

He thought of lying but dismissed the idea. She could obviously see how terrified he was.

"Yes," he answered. And asked, just for the sake of it: "Are you?"

She looked at him proudly. "Remember, I am a Zebak," she said. "Zebak never admit to fear." Then suddenly she smiled, and for a moment she reminded him of Allun. "But I am a Traveler, too." She laughed. "And as a Traveler, I say, yes, yes, yes! I am scared to death." She paused. "Travelers do not believe in lying when there is no point," she added.

Rowan felt a wave of thankfulness wash over him. At least he was not alone. He grinned back at Zeel, ignoring the pounding of his heart.

They began to walk across the small strip of flat land that separated the rocky slope from the trees. The cheerful yellow daisies in their path seemed to mock them. Trodden underfoot, they sprang back to face the sun as soon as Rowan and Zeel had passed. They were not made sad and fearful by the Pit of Unrin. They grew just as carelessly as ever up to the very rim of the trees.

But, as Rowan saw, they grew no farther. Once the trees began, there were no more clumps of grass, no more daisies. It was as though every scrap of normal life ended where Unrin began.

It was all ugliness and silence. Absolute silence. No butterflies flitted among those squat, twisted trees. No birds rustled in their branches, looking for seeds and tiny caterpillars. No lizards skittered around their roots, hunting insects. No frogs croaked amid that poisonous yellow fog.

"It is all . . . dead," whispered Zeel, pointing to the gray earth. "Not the trees, but everything else. And the smell!" She wrinkled her nose.

"Zeel . . ." Rowan hesitated. "Zeel, do we know what dangers we might face here?"

She shook her head. "Our stories do not tell us that." She bit her lip. "All they tell us is that it is a place of monsters. No living thing has ever entered Unrin and returned. It is forbidden."

It is forbidden.

"That's what they said about the Mountain," Rowan said. "And yet seven of us climbed it, and seven of us returned."

Zeel straightened her shoulders. "Then maybe it will be the same with Unrin," she said, forcing a smile. "And why not? Who knows, in these tales, what is truth and what is just imagination? And it may have suited the people of the Valley of Gold to let outsiders think Unrin is deadly."

She nodded briskly, as if to assure herself that

what she had said was true. "Come on!" she said. "We have wasted too much time already."

They turned and waved to the watching figures above them. And then they bent and moved forward, Zeel first, Rowan second, into the twisting maze that was Unrin.

Shuffling slowly along, his eyes darting everywhere, the hair prickling on the back of his neck, Rowan held his hand over his nose to try to keep back the odious smell. Fine gray dust puffed out under his feet. But underneath the dust the ground felt as hard as stone.

Within seconds they could no longer see the slope down which they had scrambled. They could no longer see the sky. The twisting trunks and branches closed in behind and above them, locking them into a dim, evil-smelling world of gray-black silence.

"Should we mark the trees?" he whispered nervously. "So we know the way back?"

"We will be able to follow our footprints in the dust," murmured Zeel. "Be still. Listen to your heart. Trust it." Her voice was tight with tension.

They walked on. For five minutes. Ten. Nothing happened. But Rowan did not relax. He kept finding that he was holding his breath. And in his mind there were pictures. Growing brighter. Growing stronger.

"It is near." Zeel's pale eyes were glowing. Her steps quickened. "The Valley of Gold. I feel it."

"I, too," said Rowan.

The silver spring, bubbling cool and fresh from beneath the earth . . . beautiful people, tall and strong, wise and good . . . flowers and fruits of every kind, spilling across the paths of gleaming gems that wound between the gardens . . . small white horses, saddled with silk . . . houses painted with beautiful patterns, each one different . . . before each house, a golden bird— an owl with emerald eyes . . .

A fabled place of good. Guarded by a place of evil.

Voices whispered to him from the past, clouding the bright pictures, piercing him with dread.

. . . a place of evil and darkness . . . a place of death . . . a place to fear. A place to dread . . .

"Do not fear, small Rowan. . . ."

"But what if it is true? What if it is? And what if one day I have to go there?"

"You will never have to go there, Rowan. I promise."

Something was watching them. Rowan could feel it. Something knew they were here. Something was waiting. Waiting . . .

His whole body shuddered with the knowledge as his eyes desperately searched the dark shadows between the trees, the twisted branches over his head, the crawling yellow fog on the ground. But there was nothing. Nothing.

Yet he knew. "Zeel!" he hissed to the hurrying figure in front of him. "Zeel—"

And then the ground shifted under his feet. The dust flew high. And he shrieked as something grabbed at his ankles, wrapping around them, pulling his feet out from under him.

He fell heavily, screaming, hearing Zeel's screams. He stared with unbelieving horror at the thrashing gray-white thing that had risen up like a great blind worm from the earth and was binding him with terrible strength in loop after loop of its whipping tail.

"Snake!" shouted Zeel, throwing herself on the creature, stabbing at it with her knife, tearing at it with her fingers.

Bands like iron tightened on Rowan's legs, his stomach, his chest. He could feel his strength leaving him as the breath was squeezed from his lungs. He was being crushed. He was being dragged toward the swollen, twisted base of a tree, where more of the great gray-white worms were rising from the dry earth, reaching for him like the tentacles of some sea monster in Ogden's tales.

A red mist of horror swept across his eyes as he realized the truth. The monsters of Unrin were not hiding in the trees. The monsters were the trees themselves. Trees that fed on living creatures. It was the roots of a tree that were dragging him in. And the tree itself seemed to be quivering, bending toward him. Wanting. Hungry.

He tried to scream in terror, but no voice came from his mouth. He felt Zeel pulling at him, trying to tear him free. And then he thought he could hear a sound. A creaking, groaning sound. The sound of something that had waited long and was going to feed at last.

His head was pressed against the base of the tree now, crushed into the dusty mass of tiny bones and the dried, shrunken bodies of birds, lizards, and other creatures that the tree had fed on while it waited for bigger game. He saw a gray-white tentacle rise up beside him and felt a hideous, evil-smelling smoothness slither over his face and mouth.

Filled with horror, hardly knowing what he was doing, he bit at the root with all his strength. It quivered, and he bit harder.

The root thrashed and struggled, pulling roughly away from him. There was a deep, growling noise from deep within the tree. Was it pain? How could it be, when Zeel's sharp knife had torn at his attacker in vain?

But the tentacle was whipping back, away from him. And with disbelief he felt and saw the others pulling away also, freeing his hands, his chest, his legs, and being sucked back into the earth. And then Zeel was hauling him to his feet, screaming at him.

"Run!" she was shrieking. "They are all around us. Run, run, run!"

17 ⌒ ESCAPE

They ran, leaping and stumbling through the dust. Roots broke through the earth ahead of them, beside them, twisting and reaching for them, till the ground seemed to writhe with gray-white snakes.

Rowan ran blindly, every breath sending shooting pains through his bruised chest.

"Come *on!*" begged Zeel. "Rowan, do not give up!"

She caught at his hand, grasping it tightly. She dragged him on with her. The air was filled with dust and the slithering, thrashing sounds of the seeking trees. Roots coiled in a mass under their feet, whipping upward, snatching at their ankles, but never quite taking hold.

Rowan knew he could not go on like this much longer. Soon he would stumble and fall. And then . . .

"Look ahead!" cried Zeel. "There is an opening here. This may be it—the way. Oh, hurry!"

They burst through the trees into a small clearing—a patch of wet, marshy ground quite different from the rest. The trees grew closely around the edges of the marsh, bending forward, locking their branches overhead.

Rowan and Zeel waded into the sticky gray mud. Pebbles and larger stones held in the ooze bruised their feet and knocked against their bodies as they struggled to the center.

They stood there together, panting and clinging to each other.

"We cannot stay here," gasped Rowan. "They know where we are. They are coming for us." He shivered all over. The mud was heaving and alive. The tree roots were slithering through it like white eels, searching for them.

"Rowan, I can see light!" Zeel screamed suddenly, and pointed.

Rowan looked up but could see nothing. Nothing but mud, and trees, and wriggling, seeking tentacles nosing toward them.

Zeel began struggling forward. "Rowan, look

ahead! Can't you see? We are nearly there! We are nearly at the end of the trees! We are nearly—" Her words were cut off by a choking scream as she was pulled down.

Rowan lunged for her. He pulled her head and shoulders out of the suffocating mud. He struggled desperately to free her from the strangling tentacle that bound her around the chest. He felt a big stone against his leg. He pulled it, dripping, out of the marsh and beat at the tentacle with it, battering it, clawing and biting it at the same time, refusing to give in.

It jerked and let go. Sobbing and choking, Zeel and Rowan flung themselves forward. Rowan looked up again. Now he, too, could see what the Forerunner's sharp eyes had seen before him. Light, glimmering faintly, ahead.

He felt the ground begin to harden under his feet. The marsh was ending. And the trees were ending, too. He could see the towering cliff face. It was shining golden in the sunlight.

"Zeel! A few more steps," he shrieked. "Zeel, come on!"

They ran forward, leaping clear of the last of the grasping tree roots, clambering up the jagged golden rocks while the roots writhed up after them, lashing and twisting. Rowan turned and beat use-lessly at them with the stone he still held in his hand.

"Don't try!" gasped Zeel. "Climb! There is a ledge higher up. We should be safe there. Don't look down. Don't look down!"

Rowan pushed his aching body on, every moment expecting to feel a lashing tug on his ankle that would send him crashing to the ground below. He saw Zeel reach the ledge and turn to him, stretching out her arm.

With the last of his strength he held up his hand and felt her pull him to safety. Then he fell back on the hard rock, and blackness closed over him.

Rowan opened his eyes and saw blue sky. He heard the sound of birds. He took a deep breath of sweet air, and winced with pain. Every bone and muscle in his body seemed bruised.

"Are you all right?" Zeel's voice was as brisk as ever, but when he looked at her, he could see that her eyes were warm.

He nodded, then shook his head. "I don't know," he said finally. He sat up, groaning, brushing peb-bles and wet filth from his arms. The big muddy stone that had been his weapon against the trees lay beside him. He picked it up and put it on his lap, patting it thankfully.

The girl watched him, her face serious. "You saved my life," she said. "My people owe you a debt."

"No, they don't," said Rowan. "You saved my life, too. We are even."

She peered over the ledge to the trees of Unrin crouched below them. "No," she answered. "You saved yourself. Nothing I did helped. It was when you bit at the tree root that it let you go."

Her pale eyes turned to him. "You are stronger than you look," she said thoughtfully. "Ogden was right to send you with me." Frowning, she began scraping pebbles from her soft shoes, black and soaked from the marsh.

Rowan rubbed the stone. It felt cool, smooth, and comforting under his fingers. He blinked at a small blue bird fluttering behind Zeel's head, picking at some berries on a bush growing from a crack in the cliff face. The bird was strange to him.

He leaned over a little to see it more clearly. And then he saw what it was feasting on. A Mountain berry bush. Now he realized what the sweet smell was.

Rin! An agonizing jab of fear ran through his

whole body. The danger he had just faced had driven everything else from his mind, but suddenly he remembered why they were here. Why they had faced the terrors of Unrin in the first place.

"Zeel," he exclaimed, trying to get up and falling back. "Zeel, how long have we been here? We have to move on. We have to find the Valley of Gold. We have to—"

Zeel shook her head. Her mud-streaked face was grim. "I am sorry, Rowan," she said gently.

"What do you mean?"

"I have called the others to come for us. I have told them we have failed."

"No!" Rowan looked around him wildly. "No! Listen! Ogden said it was here. Beyond Unrin. And a Mountain berry bush grows there, behind you. How could it have come here unless the people of the Valley of Gold brought fruit down from the Mountain long ago? Ogden said they climbed it."

"Ogden does not know everything, it seems," said Zeel.

Rowan would not give in so easily. "But we felt it was near, Zeel. You felt it, and so did I. The entrance to the Valley could be down there, anywhere along the base of this cliff! It could be—"

Zeel shook her head again. "Our visions were but

dreams made by hope and fear. The Valley of Gold is not here."

There was terrible sorrow in her face now.

"How often we have looked down from the cliff top, believing. But we were foolish to believe. From this ledge you can see the whole of the cliff face, as you cannot see it from the top. Look and see for yourself. There are no caves, no tunnels in the rock. Nothing."

Rowan hung his head so she would not see the desperation on his face. He could not believe this was happening.

Zeel's voice went on. "So the Valley of Gold was a legend all along," she said bitterly. "It never did exist. It was never going to help us. It was all a lie— a tale to amuse children around the fire."

Rowan gripped the stone, rubbing it, looking for an answer.

"Maybe it is somewhere else," he muttered. "Maybe, if we try—" He broke off, staring at the stone beneath his muddy fingers. His heart pounded, and he gave a strangled cry.

"What is wrong?" asked Zeel sharply, dropping her shoes and starting to her feet.

Rowan looked at the cliff face, glimmering gold. He looked down at the evil trees of Unrin and the stone in his lap. He reached out with trembling fingers and took a handful of muddy pebbles from the ledge, picked others from his own clothes, rubbed them between his hands. And as he saw bright, flashing color shine through the black coating, a wave of pain washed over him, and he bent double, hunching over on the ground.

"Rowan, what *is* it?" the girl shrieked. "Have you gone mad? All right, so we have not found the Valley of Gold. So Ogden was wrong about everything. So it was a legend after all. And this is sad for all of us." Her voice began to tremble. "But we must face it, as the others must. And we can still try to help your people—"

"Ogden was not wrong about everything," Rowan breathed. "*You* are wrong, Zeel. The Valley of Gold is not a legend. We have found it."

Zeel stared at him, shaking her head in disbelief and fear.

"We have found it," Rowan repeated, staring down at the twisted mass of black trees below. "We have seen its golden wall. We huddle on it now. We have walked its jeweled paths. Their gems are sticking to our shoes and clothes. We have crossed its silver spring. Its mud and ooze still cling to us."

He held up the big stone. Cleaned of the sticky

mud, its shape was clear, and streaks of its true color glinted in the sun. It was a golden owl with emerald eyes.

Rowan took a deep, shuddering breath. "The Pit of Unrin does not guard the Valley of Gold, Zeel," he said. "The two are one and the same."

18 ∽ "AND WHEN AT LAST ITS FACE IT SHOWS . . ."

"I do not understand!" Zeel shook her head over and over again, looking at the gems slipping through her fingers and then staring down at the dark mass of Unrin. "How could this have happened? Why did no one know of it?"

"It happened long ago," said Rowan, remembering the stories. "The Travelers were on the coast, fighting the Zebak. They returned after years away. The new place they called the Pit of Unrin was here. The Valley they knew had disappeared. And by chance rocks had fallen from the Mountain to make everything look different. Perhaps they made up the story of the Giants of Inspray to explain it. Who knows?"

"But the people of the Valley!" exclaimed Zeel.

"They were supposed to be so clever and so wise. How could they let their home be overtaken by such an enemy? How could they? How did the trees come here and take hold in so short a time?"

She paced along the ledge, putting up her hand to feel the wind. "It is changing," she said abruptly, stuffing the shining gems into her pockets. "Come. We must climb to the top of the cliff to await the Forerunners."

Rowan picked up the golden owl and tucked it into his shirt. As he clambered to his feet he caught sight of a patch of blue beneath the Mountain berry bush. He moved closer to investigate.

It was the bird. It was lying very still, its eyes closed, its tiny beak open. The feathers on its chest fluffed softly as it breathed. It was fast asleep.

The rich perfume of the Mountain berry flowers drifted sweetly on the air. The luscious red berries winked temptingly.

"The Mountain berries," whispered Rowan. In his mind he saw the birds of Rin, lying still, like this, on the grass. He saw the people huddled on streets and in gardens. The people who had breathed in the scent of those sweet red flowers as they bloomed everywhere in Rin, more every day. More and more . . .

"Zeel!" he gasped, spinning around to face her. "My people—it is the Mountain berry flowers that are putting them to sleep. The scent of the flowers! Look at that bird."

She looked curiously at the sleeping bird, then moved closer, touching it with a gentle finger.

"Who would have thought it?" she murmured, shaking her head. She glanced up at Rowan's anxious face and grinned.

"Rowan, don't look so worried," she said. "Do you not realize what this means? It means that our journey through Unrin was not wasted. It means that the answer *did* lie here, after all!"

She jumped up and clasped his hand. "Do not fear!" she cried. "The bird is sleeping, not dead. And your people are sleeping, too. All we have to do is go back to Rin and pull out the Mountain berry bushes, or at least most of them. And then the sleeping sickness will be gone."

Rowan frowned doubtfully.

Zeel put her hands on her hips and stared at him in irritation. "I do not understand you!" she shouted. "You should be rejoicing! Your problem is solved! And no wonder the Mountain berries were the cause of your trouble. The Mountain is forbidden. It is full of strange, monstrous things we cannot even imagine."

"I am just not sure, Zeel," mumbled Rowan, watching the sleeping bird. "I am not sure we have the whole answer. It is the rhyme. Sheba's rhyme. It doesn't fit. She spoke of a great evil, a secret enemy, whose power grows in darkness. It cannot be these little bushes. Or a sleeping sickness so easily cured. There must be something else."

He repeated the chant under his breath.

> "The secret enemy is here.
> It hides in darkness, fools beware!
> For day by day its power grows,
> And when at last its face it shows,
> Then past and present tales will meet—
> The evil circle is complete."

Beneath soft looks the evil burns . . . It hides in darkness . . . day by day its power grows, And when at last its face it shows . . .

Something stirred in Rowan's mind. An idea, fluttering just where he could not see it clearly. He blinked, trying to catch at it. And then he saw himself, standing in the bukshah fields with Star, thinking about the Travelers and the changes of spring, watching the butterfly crawl from its cocoon.

He heard Annad's voice. "Why? Why do tadpoles eat weed, but frogs eat insects? Why . . . ?"

Tired of waiting, Zeel sighed with impatience. Then she pointed at the sky. Two kites, one yellow, one red, were wheeling against the blue.

"Tor and Mithren are coming," she cried. "We must go. Wait—I will get the bird. It will starve if we leave it sleeping here."

Things change, Annad, thought Rowan. Nature is strange and wonderful. One sort of creature can become another, in a season. Adult creatures can be quite different from their children—with different looks, different appetites, different . . .

His eyes widened. Tadpoles and frogs. Caterpillars and butterflies.

Zeel bent to pick up the small bundle of feathers beneath the Mountain berry bush.

"Zeel!" shouted Rowan. "Come away!"

And at that moment the ground beneath their feet began to rumble and shudder. Zeel cried out in shock, falling back with the bird in her hand and nearly knocking Rowan off the ledge.

"What is happening?" she screamed, clutching Rowan in terror.

Pieces of golden rock began to crack from the cliff face below the Mountain berry bush, falling and smashing to the ground far below. The cliff was cracking open. The Mountain berry bush was thrashing wildly, its berries and flowers tumbling from its branches as it was pushed up and up out of the rock by something huge and powerful beneath.

"Climb!" shouted Rowan. "Climb!"

And when at last its face it shows . . .

Zeel thrust the bird inside her jacket and they began to scramble upward, their fingers straining, their feet scrabbling on the rock.

"What *is* it?" panted Zeel, looking back.

"It is the enemy," gasped Rowan. "The enemy! Showing its face. Zeel—it is one of them. One of the Unrin trees. The Mountain berry bushes—they are just the young form of those trees down there. The adults grow underneath them. The bushes collect the trees' first food, with their scent. They—"

With a hideous sound of splitting rock, a squat black shape rose up beneath the tiny bush that crowned it. Its gray-white roots, like thick, twisting worms, slithered around the ground, looking for food—the food they expected to find.

Zeel clutched her jacket. "I have the bird," she shouted at the tree. "I have it! You will have to go hungry!"

The roots began to feel their way up the cliff face. Reaching for them.

"Climb!" cried Rowan desperately.

They heaved their way up the cliff. Rowan looked up, trying to forget the tearing pains in his legs and chest, trying to forget the awful drop below. He saw Tor and Mithren looking down, helplessly holding out their arms. He could hear the roots of the Unrin tree slapping the rock behind him and the grating sound of more stone splitting away as the adult tree reached up and out, released at last from the darkness of the earth.

Gasping and panting he climbed, and in his mind was only one horrible vision. The valley of Rin, changed utterly to a hideous maze of twisted trees and dried gray earth. Its houses and lanes crushed under reaching black branches and tentaclelike roots. Its sleeping people locked to the bases of the feeding trees, their lives slowly ebbing away.

Then past and present tales will meet—
The evil circle is complete.

No! He would not let the circle be completed. He would not let Rin be destroyed as the Valley of Gold had been. He would not let its people, *his* people, disappear, as so long ago another race had vanished. This time it would be stopped. This time . . .

Tor's hand grasped his wrist and pulled him over the cliff edge. Rowan saw gentle hills and plains, with grass and slip-daisies stretching to the horizon. The golden owl fell from his shirt and tumbled onto the ground. He stood swaying, watching Zeel crumpling beside him.

She lay still, panting and exhausted. Then she thrust her hand inside her jacket and brought out the bird. It had woken. It sat on her palm for a moment, and then, in a flash of blue, it was fluttering free.

"Good," Zeel groaned, with a spark of her old fierceness. "Fly away. And let the devil tree go hungry."

"Zeel, get up," Rowan urged her. "We must go! We must go to Rin!"

19 ∽ HURRY!

They flew. Rowan with Zeel, Allun with Tor, and with Mithren—Ogden.

It had taken only moments to glide back to the waiting Travelers. Only moments to tell the tale. Only moments for Ogden to give his orders and for the third kite to be made ready.

But every second was agony to Rowan. In his mind he saw his mother and Jonn lying helpless on the grass outside Bree and Hanna's house. He saw Annad asleep inside. And Lann. And, sprawled on lanes, in gardens, on their own doorsteps, the other people he had known all his life. While all the time the enemy grew in darkness and the Mountain berries bloomed.

How long did it take for the adult tree to grow

strong enough to emerge? With a shudder he remembered Bree's voice. "But the ground was hard—like iron, it seemed." Hard, so hard—not because of magic, as they had thought, but because the adult tree was growing there, secret and safe, making itself ready. . . .

Faster, faster, he thought, willing the wind to speed the kite on. And yet, he realized with a feeling of panic that trembled on the edge of despair, he did not know what he would find when he got to Rin.

"Nearly there," cried Zeel, her voice almost lost in the wind. "We will land on the hills, where it is clear."

Rowan looked down and saw golden hills, and ahead, the valley. Gone was the brown-and-green patchwork. Now Rin was a carpet of red blossoms.

The Mountain berries had spread—astonishingly fast. They were everywhere: in the gardens, the lanes, the fields, the orchard. The great stone mill stood alone in a sea of red, the bukshah pool was surrounded by a scarlet band that spread right to the orchard.

"Zeel, what will we do?" he shouted in despair.

Her fierce black-browed face turned to him, and in her pale eyes he saw the remorseless rage of a

Zebak warrior. "Thank the stars that they have not yet spread out of the valley," she shouted. "Now it will be easy to do what we decided. We will burn them, Rowan. Burn them! Burn them!"

They ran down the hill together. Pollen from the slip-daisies blew into Rowan's face, and he sneezed, tears running down his cheeks. But never again would he curse the daisies, he promised himself. Sweet, happy, wild things, they had been weeded out in Rin because they were useless. But the Mountain berries had been welcomed because they were a source of pride and riches. The people of the Valley of Gold had probably felt the same way when they had brought their own handfuls of Mountain berries down from the Mountain in triumph.

The same mistakes, the same old pride.

The rhyme made sense now. All but one line. Rowan thought about that as they reached the grove of trees where he had met Sheba. The memory of her words rang in his ears. Still one mystery. Still—

"There!" shouted Zeel savagely, pointing at a froth of red shining under one of the trees. She picked up a stick covered in dead leaves and lit it.

"No, not here, not yet," cried Allun, racing past

her. "The people. We have to get the people out first! My mother, Marlie, Jiller, Jonn . . . oh, so many. We must hurry! Hurry!"

"It will only take a moment," Zeel shouted after him, throwing the flaming leaves into the center of the Mountain berry bushes. "A moment to get these devils and— Oh!"

Her scream stopped them in their tracks, made them turn and look. They saw flames, leaping among the berry plants. Then they saw the flames hissing and dying. They saw the ground breaking and cracking, clods of earth and clumps of grass falling.

And they saw the trees rising—huge, swollen, black as night. Their roots, as thick as giant snakes, thrashed out, whipping through the air toward Zeel, toward them, toward any living creature they could snare and drag in.

"Run! Run!" Rowan heard his own voice screaming as in horror he saw Zeel leaping for her life— away from the trees, away from the writhing tentacles that were hunting her.

She reached his side, her face white. "The fire," she gasped. "As soon as it hit the plants, the adults broke out. It must anger them. And they are huge, Rowan. So much bigger than the trees of Unrin."

"The ground is far richer here," said Ogden grimly.

Allun was trembling. "Marlie and I saw nothing like that on the Mountain," he said. "Nothing at all. There were some small, twisted trees behind the bushes where I picked the berries, but . . ."

Ogden rubbed his chin. "On the Mountain, rock lies just beneath the soil, and cold winds blow. There this cursed plant must remain stunted, preying on insects and other crawling creatures. But here—as in the Valley of Gold—there will be no stopping it."

Rowan stood frozen. The flames in which they had placed such hope were useless. And there was no other way he could think of to save the valley.

Allun grabbed his arm. "We must get our people out," he said urgently. "It is our only chance now. We will have to get them out—as many as we can. Before—before—"

He could not go on.

Ogden's brow was deeply creased. "There must be a way," he muttered. "There is always a way. The land knows. It protects its creatures. It keeps the balance."

"Not this time," cried Allun. "Because these *things* are from the Mountain. Thanks to me, they are here!" Tears sprang into his eyes. "I cannot wait for you!" he shouted.

He ran toward the village. Zeel, Tor, and Mithren ran with him.

But Rowan stayed where he was, with Ogden.

"The Mountain is also part of the land," Ogden said to him. "And there must be a way."

They heard distant shouting, but they did not move.

"Say the rhyme, Rowan," Ogden commanded.

Rowan swallowed, and began.

> "Beneath soft looks the evil burns,
> And slowly round the old wheel turns.
> The same mistakes, the same old pride,
> The priceless armor cast aside—"

"Stop!" Ogden held up his hand. " 'The priceless armor cast aside,' " he repeated. "What does that mean?"

"I don't know," Rowan whispered desperately. "I have been trying and *trying* to understand it. But it doesn't mean anything to me. It seems a nonsense. Yet everything else in the rhyme is important. Everything!"

"And so must this be," said Ogden. "Rowan, think! Somewhere in you is the clue to this. It is buried deep, perhaps, but it is there. Because you are special. Something about you is special. *You* escaped the sleeping sickness and saved Allun from it. *You* saved yourself, and Zeel, in the Pit of Unrin. You alone have done these things. How? Why?"

"I don't know! I don't know!" cried Rowan, burying his face in his hands. Like a mocking echo he heard Sheba's sneering voice. "Skinny rabbit! Weakling, runny-nosed child, scared of your own shadow! No use to your mother in her need. . . . No use to anyone . . . weakling, runny-nosed child, weakling, runny-nosed . . ."

He gasped. He saw himself dragging Allun out of Rin, out into the hills. He remembered biting and tearing at the strangling roots of the Unrin trees. He remembered something Jonn had said. He remembered Zeel: "Thank the stars that they have not yet spread out of the valley." He remembered Sheba, eyes glazed: "I only know that I must work."

He spun around to Ogden. "The plants *couldn't* get out of the valley!" he shouted. "Because the hills still have their armor on. Their golden armor. Their priceless armor. Like me. Don't you see?"

Ogden stared at him.

"Call the others!" Rowan cried. "I know what we need. And I know where to get it. It is ready. It is waiting for us. Ogden, please!"

Ogden wasted no time with questions. He put his reed pipe to his lips and blew.

20 ∽ AN END, AND A BEGINNING

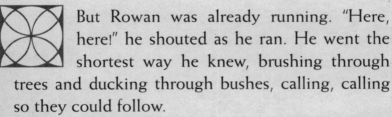

But Rowan was already running. "Here, here!" he shouted as he ran. He went the shortest way he knew, brushing through trees and ducking through bushes, calling, calling so they could follow.

Dozens of Mountain berry bushes clustered around the low door of Sheba's hut. They were big. They were ready. Mice, lizards, and birds lay waiting to be devoured. And inside, something bigger.

Rowan burst into the hut. Like a bundle of old rags and straggled hair, Sheba lay huddled by the cold fire. He leaped past her, to the great iron pot that hung over the dead coals. It was filled to the brim with oily, foul-smelling liquid. Rowan took a ladleful and sipped. Yes!

"Rowan! Are you there? Rowan!"

He ran to the doorway. Ogden and the Forerunners were standing there.

"Look!" shouted Rowan. He tipped a few drops of liquid from his ladle over the plants at his feet. They quivered and drooped. The ground heaved. And then, as Zeel, Tor, and Mithren screamed, the hideous, familiar black trunks appeared, pushing, twisting, reaching out.

The Forerunners fell back. But Rowan did not move. He let a few more drops of the brew of the slip-daisy roots fall onto the writhing things. And then they shuddered and turned back on themselves, and finally, with a horrible seething sigh, split from end to end, and lay still.

"The slip-daisies," Rowan choked. "They are the armor. Jonn told Annad that other plants don't thrive where slip-daisies grow. So we weeded them out. Every one. And the people of the Valley of Gold—they would have done it, too. To make their orchards, and build their houses, and pave their jeweled paths. So when the Mountain berries came, they were defenseless. Just like us."

He held up the ladle. "But this—this potion is made from slip-daisy roots. I have been drinking it all along. I am the only one who has. I am full of it, so the trees could not take me. It kills them. It kills them!"

The Forerunners ran toward him.

"There is lots more," he gabbled. "Sheba made it. She knew. She knew she had to. But she didn't know why. Inside! Quickly!"

"Fill the bottles with it," ordered Ogden. "Take the kites. Drop the liquid on the village first, then on the fields. Be sparing. Do not waste any. Rowan, take jugs, bowls, anything! We will go on foot."

"My mother!" gasped Rowan. "My sister! At the gardens!"

The gardens seethed with gray-white snakes. They crept across the grass, coiled in Jiller's hair, felt for Jonn. The trees leaned forward, breaking through the fencing, reaching for the house where other flesh lay sleeping.

Rowan ran among them, shouting, hurling the precious liquid at them, watching with savage pleasure as they split and withered, and their roots fell lifeless on the grass.

Ogden let him go and went on his way, quietly pouring the liquid from his jug here and there, wherever it was needed, watching the kites dipping and wheeling and his young people doing their work over the town.

He understood how the boy felt. He knew what it meant to defend a home. The whole land was his home. And he had fought for it, in his time. But never quite like this, he thought. There has never been an enemy quite like this.

Then he corrected himself. But, of course, there had. He was forgetting the circle. Long, long ago, the same ancient enemy had come down from the Mountain. And then it had won.

"But not this time," he said aloud, tipping his jug. He watched three drops fall and the pretty, sweet-smelling little plant at his feet droop and die. "This time, a boy with the sniffles beat you."

He paused. He watched a sleeping mouse by his foot stir, sit up, clean its whiskers in surprise, then scuttle away. He smiled as he saw it go. He was thinking of the story he would tell.

The flames of the fire leaped high. The children listened, wide-eyed.

Ogden the storyteller leaned forward, his lean face ghostly and shadowed. "And Rowan took the liquid from the witch's cauldron, and he ran, shouting like a wild man, shouting with a hundred voices, right into the midst of the ravenous trees that writhed and spat at him."

Jiller squeezed Rowan's arm. Jonn put his hand on his shoulder. Annad nestled closer to him. "Was that how it was, Rowan?" she breathed.

He shrugged. It was not *quite* as he remembered it. But he was not going to spoil a good story. Not yet, anyway. He was too happy. Too relieved. Too filled with joy.

He grinned at Allun, standing near Ogden with his arms around Sara and Marlie. He knew no one blamed Allun for what had happened. Everyone took the blame equally. They had said so. And Allun had been greeted as a hero, for joining with him in finding the Travelers and fighting the enemy.

He grinned at Zeel, smiling at him over the leaping flames. He saw Neel the potter, and Bree and Hanna with Maise and all their children. He saw Bronden, Val and Ellis, Timon, Lann. And all the others. Everyone was there. Everyone but Sheba, who cursed them all as fools and stumped back to her hut.

The months ahead would be hard. There would be much work to do, repairing the damage done to the village by the trees of Unrin. Food would be scarce. New crops would have to be planted. But everyone was rejoicing. Just to be alive.

Ogden's voice was rising.

"And Rowan spattered them with the brew once, twice, three times," he shouted. "They screamed, and twisted, and split open—and died." He paused, looking around him. His voice dropped to a low murmur. "And their coiling roots, tangled still in his mother's hair, just withered and crumbled away. Useless. Helpless. Dead."

There was a breathless hush.

"And all around the village Allun and the Travelers were doing their work, and the other plants of evil were dying. So by sunset the village was safe. The bukshah had returned. The people had woken. And so had the birds, and the bukshah calves, and all the other creatures that had so nearly been swallowed up and destroyed by the trees of Unrin. The valley was alive again. The wheel had been stopped. The old story had a new ending. The circle had been broken.

"And the people of Rin rejoiced, and sang, and were happy. For a while, they cared nothing for riches. For once, they were like the Travelers. Just happy to breathe the air. To look at the sky. And

that night, when the moon was full, Ogden the storyteller told a tale. A tale he would tell over and
over again, across the land, for many years to
come."

He leaned back. "It was a tale of courage and
fear; of legend and truth; of a puzzle and an
answer; of suspicion and friendship; of a treasure
lost, and another treasure saved; of a terrible
enemy who came not from outside, but from
within."

He smiled. "And most of all it was the tale of a
skinny rabbit with a runny nose and a great heart,
who came back to save his home and would not
stop until it was done."

The people started to cheer and clap. The sound
went on for minutes. It roared through the valley. It
echoed from the Mountain. It floated across the
hills to where the Travelers' carts trundled quietly
back to Rin.

And when the sound had finally died, Ogden
stood up.

"There is one more thing," he said.

He took a silk bag from Zeel. He walked slowly
around the fire, to Rowan.

"Your people owe you a debt," he said. "But so do

we. You saved the life of our beloved adopted daughter Zeel, and for that you only have to call on us, and we will come to you. From anywhere. At any time. This is our solemn promise."

He handed Rowan a reed pipe.

Rowan stammered his thanks.

"And," added Ogden casually, putting his hand back into the bag, "you left these behind, at our camp. We return them to you now. The village may find a use for them, in the months to come."

The precious gems fell from his fingers into Rowan's lap like many-colored raindrops. There was a gasp from the crowd. Ogden's black eyes glittered. His arm dipped back into the bag. And into Rowan's hands he put the golden owl. It had been cleaned and polished. It shone like the sun. Its eyes were green fire.

"Sell the rest, but keep this," he said. "Like me, it is very old, very precious, and has many stories to tell. Keep this, Rowan of the Bukshah, as a sign of our friendship. It is the only one of its kind now. For we will not seek to clear the Pit of Unrin, and uncover the sad bones and lost glories of the Valley of Gold. The time of that golden place has ended. As the time of Rin has just begun."

Amid a stunned silence he walked back to the fire and sat down. "Now!" he said, looking around and plumping his hands on his knees. "Could anyone spare a poor, useless Slip some dinner?"

And there wasn't a person there who didn't run to do his bidding.